The Ethical Engineer

Harry Harrison

The Ethical Engineer

The present edition is a reproduction of previous publication of this classic work. Minor typographical errors may have been corrected without note; however, for an authentic reading experience the spelling, punctuation, and capitalization have been retained from the original text.

ISBN: 979-8-88830-668-0

All nature is but art, unknown to thee;
All chance, direction which thou canst not see;
All discord, harmony not understood;
All partial evil, universal good:
And, spite of pride, in erring reasons spite,
One truth is clear, Whatever is, is right.

Alexander Pope
Essay on Man

I

Jason dinAlt looked unhappily at the two stretchers as they were carried by. "Are they at it again?" he asked.

Brucco nodded, the scowl permanently ingrained now on his hawklike face. "We have only one thing to be thankful for. That is—so far at least—they haven't used any weapons on each other."

Jason looked down unbelievingly at the shredded clothing, crushed flesh and broken bones. "The absence of weapons doesn't appear to make much difference when two Pyrrans start fighting. It seems impossible that this damage could be administered bare-handed."

"Well it was. Even you should know that much about Pyrrus by now. We take our fighting very seriously. But they never think how much more work it makes for me. Now I have to patch these two idiots up and try to find room for them in the ward." He stalked away, irritated and annoyed as always. Jason usually laughed at the doctor's irascible state, but not today.

Today, and for some days past, he had found himself living with a persistent feeling of irritation, that had arrived at the same time as his discovery that it is far easier to fight a war than to administer a peace. The battle at the perimeter still continued, since the massed malevolence of the Pyrran life forms were not going to call a truce simply because the two warring groups of humans had done so. There was battle on the perimeter and a continual feeling of unrest inside the city. So far there had been very little traffic between the city Pyrrans and those living outside the walls, and what contact there had been usually led to the kind of violence he had just witnessed. The only minor note of hope in this concert of discord was the fact that no one had died—as yet—in any of these fearsome hand-to-hand conflicts. In spite of the apparent deadliness of the encounters all of the Pyrrans seemed to understand that, despite past hatreds, they were all really on the same side. A distant rumble from the clouded sky broke through his thoughts.

"There is a ship on the radar," Meta said, coming out of the ground-control office and squinting up at the overcast. "I wonder if it is that ecology expedition that Brucco arranged—or the cargo ship from Ondion?"

"We'll find out in a few minutes," Jason said, happy to forget his troubles for the moment in frank admiration, since just looking at Meta was enough to put a golden edge on this gloom-filled day. Standing there, head back searching the sky, she managed to be beautiful even in the formless Pyrran coverall. Jason put his arms around her waist and exacted a great deal of pleasure from kissing the golden length of her up-stretched throat.

"Oh, Jason ... not now," she said in exasperation. Pyrran minds, by necessity, run along one track at a time, and at the present moment she was thinking about the descending spaceship. With a quick motion, scarcely aware of her action, she pulled his hands from her and pushed him away, an easy enough thing for a Pyrran girl to do. But in doing so she half fractured one of his wrists, numbed the other, and knocked Jason to the ground.

"Darling ... I'm sorry," she gasped, suddenly realizing what she had done, bending quickly to help him up.

"Get away, you lady weight-lifter," he growled, pushing aside the proffered hand and struggling to his feet. "When are you going to realize that I'm only human, not made of chrome steel bars like the rest of your people...." He stifled the rest of his words in disgust, at himself, his temper, this deadly planet and the cantankerousness of its citizens that was scratching away at his nerves. He turned and stamped away, angry at himself for taking out his vile mood on Meta, but still too annoyed to make peace.

Meta watched him leave, trying to say something that would end this foolish quarrel, but unable to. The largest blank in the Pyrran personality was an almost complete lack of knowledge of human nature, and her struggle to fill in the gaps—gaps she was only just beginning to realize existed—was a difficult one. The stronger emotions of hate and fear were no strangers to her; but for the first time she was discovering how difficult and complex was this unusual feeling of love. She let Jason go because she was incapable of any other action. Of course she could stop him by force, but if she had learned anything in the past few weeks, it was the discovery that this was one area where he was very sensitive. There was no doubt that she was far stronger than he—physically—and he did not like to be reminded about it. She went back into the ground-control room, almost eager to deal with the impersonal faces of the dials and scopes, material and unchanging entities that posed no conflicting problems.

***

Jason stood at the edge of the field and watched the ship come in for a landing, his anger forgotten temporarily in the presence of this break in routine. Perhaps this was the shipful of scientific eggheads that Brucco was expecting; he hoped so. It would be a pleasant treat to have a conversation with someone about a topic more universal than the bore dimensions of guns. With practiced eye he watched the landing which was a little sloppy, either a new pilot or an old one who didn't care much. It was a small ship so not many people would be aboard. Then the spacer turned for a moment, in a landing correction, and he had a quick glimpse of a serial number and tantalizingly familiar insignia on its stern—where had he seen that before?

The ship touched down and the flaring rockets died. There was only the click of cooling metal from the ship: no one emerged, nor did any of the Pyrrans seem interested enough in the newcomer to approach it. That must mean that no one had any business with it, and, of course, no curiosity either, for this along with imagination was in very short supply on the war-torn planet. Since no one else was making any moves, Jason went forward to investigate for himself.

A stingwing that had escaped the perimeter guards dived towards him and he blasted it automatically with his gun. The corpse thudded to the ground and the soil churned around it as the insectile scavengers fought for the flesh; only bare bones remained by the time he had taken two paces.

4

A muffled whine of motors told him that the lower hatch was opening, and Jason watched as a hairline crack appeared in the thick metal, then widened as the heavy door ground outwards. Through the opening he had a glimpse of a figure muffled in a heavy-duty spacesuit. That must be Meta's work, she would have contacted the ship by radio while it was on its way down and explained the standing orders that no off-worlders were to be allowed out of their ships unless wearing the heaviest armor. Since the armed truce between the human inhabitants there had been a lessening of the relentless warfare the Pyrran life forms waged against the city, but only to a slight degree. Deadly beasts still abounded, and the air was thick with toxic diseases. A stranger, unprotected, would be ill in five minutes, dead within ten—or much sooner if a horndevil or other beast got to him in the interval.

Jason felt a justified pride that he could walk this planet under his own power. The natives, adapted to the deadliness and heavy gravity since birth, were still his superiors, but he was the only off-worlder who could stand the dangers of Pyrrus. His gun whined out of his power holster into his waiting hand as he searched for some target to use his talents on. An armored piece of nastiness, with a lot of legs, was crawling into hiding under a rock and he blasted it neatly with a single shot. The gun snapped back into the holster and he turned to the open door of the spacer, his morale greatly improved.

***

"Welcome to Pyrrus," he told the ungainly figure that clumped out of the ship. There was a hefty maser-projector clutched in the armored gloves and whoever was inside the suit, the face was invisible behind the thick and tinted faceplate, seemed exceedingly nervous, turning to look in all directions.

"Don't worry," Jason said, fighting to keep a tone of smug satisfaction out of his voice, "I'll take care of things for you. I don't know what kind of horror stories you may have heard about Pyrrus—but they're all true. That's a nice looking heat ray you have there, but I doubt if you could move fast enough to use it."

The figure lowered the gun and fumbled for a switch on the front of the space armor, it clicked and a speaker diaphragm rustled.

"I'm looking for a man called Jason dinAlt. Can you tell me if he is on this planet or if he has left?"

It was impossible to tell the speaker's tone from the rasping diaphragm, and no face was visible that might betray an emotion. This was the moment when Jason should have shown caution, and have remembered that there were thousands of policemen scattered across the galaxy who would heartily enjoy putting him under arrest. Yet he couldn't imagine any of them going to the trouble of following him here. And certainly there could be very little danger from a spacesuited man with a rifle, not to the man who had learned to take Pyrrus on its own terms, and live.

"I'm Jason dinAlt," he said. "What do you want me for?"

"I've come a long way to find you," the speaker rasped. "Now"—the gloved hand pointed—"what is THAT?"

Jason's reactions were instantaneous, conditioned to move without thought. He wheeled, crouched, the gun in his hand and finger quivering lightly on the trigger, pointed in the indicated direction. There was nothing unusual to be seen, just an empty field and the control building at the edge.

"Whatever are you talking about ..." Jason asked, then stopped as it became very obvious what the stranger had been talking about. The large, flanged mouth of the maser-projector ground into the small of his back. His own gun snapped halfway out of its holster, buzzed briefly, then slipped back as he realized his position.

"That's much better," the stranger said. "If you attempt to move, turn, lower your gun hand or do anything I don't like I'll pull this trigger and...."

"I know," Jason sighed, careful to stand with every muscle frozen. "You will pull the trigger and burn a nice round hole through my backbone and intestines. But I would just like to know why? Who is it that is so interested in my worthless old carcass that they were willing to pay interstellar freight charges to send you and that oversize toaster all the way here in order to threaten it?"

Jason was only talking to kill time, since he knew this situation would not stay static for long, not on Pyrrus. He was completely right because before he had finished the ground-control door burst open and Meta ran out, circling to the left. At the same moment Kerk appeared from behind the building, his Pyrran reflexes absorbing the situation in an instant and with no perceptible delay he ran in the opposite direction. Both Pyrrans had their guns ready and closed in with the merciless precision of trained predators.

"Tell them to stop," the suit speaker grated at Jason. "I'll shoot you if they try anything."

"Hold it!" Jason shouted, and the running Pyrrans stopped instantly. "Don't come any closer and whatever you do don't shoot." He half-turned his head and spoke in a quieter voice to the suited figure behind him. "Now you see where you stand. Lower the gun and get back into your ship, I guarantee you'll stay alive if you do that at once."

"Don't try and buff me, dinAlt," the maser barrel pushed harder against his back. "You are my prisoner and your friends can't save you. Start walking backwards now—I'll stay right behind you."

"Look," Jason said calmly, not permitting himself to get angry. "Those are *Pyrrans* out there. Either of them could kill you so quickly that you couldn't possibly have time to pull that trigger. I'm saving your life—though I don't know why I'm bothering—so be a good boy and get back into your ship and go home and we'll give you a T for trying."

"Could I have him, please Kerk?" Meta called out, the deadly assumption of her remark punctuating Jason's logic. "After all, Jason means more to me than you. Shall I kill him yet, Jason?"

"Just shoot his gun hand off, Meta," Kerk told her, in the same emotionless tone. "I want to know who this is, why he came here, before he dies."

"Get back into your ship, you fool," Jason hissed. "You've got only seconds to live."

"Start walking backwards," his captor said. "You are under arrest. I'll count to three, then shoot. One ... two...."

Jason shuffled a cautious step to the rear and the Pyrran guns snapped up at the same instant, extended at arm's length. Jason was so close to the man in the spacesuit that the guns could have been pointed at him, the eyes sighting carefully over the dark muzzles.

"Don't shoot!" Jason shouted to his friends.

"Don't worry," Kerk called back. "We won't hit you."

"I know that—it's this idiot here that I'm worrying about. You just can't shoot him for trying to do his job. In fact I'm surprised to find out that there is one honest cop left on any of the places I've been."

"Don't talk so crazy," Meta said with maddening sweetness. "We'll kill him, Jason. We'll take care of you."

Anger hit him. "You will NOT take care of me because I can take care of myself. Either of you kill him and so help me I'll kill you." Jason shuffled backwards faster now until his legs hit the lower edge of the hatch. He clambered into it and burst out laughing at the dumfounded expressions of his friends' faces. The laugh died as something pricked the back of his neck. The pressure of the gun was gone and he swung around, surprised to see the floor rushing up towards him, but before it struck him blackness descended.

Consciousness returned, accompanied by a thudding headache that made Jason wince when he moved, and when he opened his eyes the pain of the light made him screw them shut again. Whatever the drug was that had knocked him out, it was fast working, and seemed to be oxidized just as quickly. The headache faded away to a dull throb and he could open his eyes without feeling that needles were being driven into them. He was seated in a standard spacechair that had been equipped with wrist and ankle locks, now well secured. A man sat in the chair next to him, intent on the spaceship's controls; the ship was in flight and well into space. The stranger was working the computer, cutting a tape to control their flight in jump-space.

Jason took the opportunity to study the man. He seemed to be a little old for a policeman, though on second thought it was really hard to tell his age. His hair was gray and cropped as short as a skull cap, but the wrinkles on his leathery skin seemed to have been caused more by exposure than advanced years. Tall and firmly erect, he appeared underweight at first glance, until Jason realized this effect was caused by the total absence of any excess flesh. It was as though he had been cooked by the sun and leeched by the rain until only bone, tendon and muscle were left. When he turned his head the muscles stood out like cables under the skin of his neck and his hands at the controls were the browned talons of some bird. A hard finger pressed the switch that actuated the jump control, and he turned away from the board to face Jason.

"I see you are awake. It was a mild drug. I did not enjoy using it, but it was the safest way."

When he talked his jaw opened and shut with the seriousness of a bank vault. The deep-set and cold blue eyes stared fixedly from under dark brows. Jason stared back just as steadily and chuckled.

"I suppose you didn't enjoy using the maser-projector either, nor threatening to cook holes in me. For a cop you seem to be very tender hearted."

"I did it only to save your friends. I did not want them to get hurt."

"Get hurt!" Jason roared with laughter. "Space-cop, don't you have any idea what Pyrrans are like, or what kind of a setup you were walking into? Don't you realize that I saved your life—though I really don't know why. Call me a natural humanitarian. You may have a swollen head and a ready trigger-finger, but you were so far out of your class that you just weren't in the race. They could have blasted you into pieces, then shot the pieces into smaller pieces, while you were still thinking about pulling the trigger. You should just thank me for being your savior."

"So you are a liar as well as a thief," Jason's captor answered with no change of expression. "You attempt to play on my sympathies to gain your freedom. Why should I believe this story? I came to arrest you, threatening to kill you if you didn't submit, and your friends were there ready to defend you. Why should you attempt to save my life? It does not make sense." He turned back to the controls to make an adjustment.

Mikah Samon

It didn't make sense, Jason agreed completely. Why had he saved this oaf who meant nothing to him? It was not an easy question to answer, though it had seemed so right at the time. If only Meta hadn't said that they would take care of him; he knew they could and was tired of it. He could take care of himself: he felt the anger rising again at the remembered words. Was that the only reason he had let this cop capture him? To show the Pyrrans that he was able to control his own destiny? Was the human ego such a pitiable thing that it had to keep reassuring itself of its own independence or lie down on its back and curl up its toes?

Apparently it was. At least his was. The years had taught him a certain insight into his own personality and he realized that his greedy little subconscious had collected all the cues and signals from the encounter at the spaceport and goaded him into a line of action that looked uncomfortably like suicide. The arrival of the stranger, the threat to himself, the automatic assumption by the Pyrrans that they would take care of him. Apparently his ego and his subconscious felt that he had been taken care of too long. They had managed to get him into this spot from which he could only be extricated by his own talents, far away from Pyrrus and the pressures that had been weighing on him so long.

He took a deep breath and smiled. It wasn't such a bad idea after all. Stupid in retrospect, but the stupidity could hopefully be kept in the past. Now he had to prove that there was something other than a death wish in his subconscious flight from Pyrrus, and he must find a way to reverse positions with this cop, whoever he was. Which meant that he had to find out a little more about the man before making any plans.

"I'm afraid you have the advantage of me, officer. How about telling me who you are and showing me a warrant or something under which you are performing this deed of interstellar justice."

"I am Mikah Samon. I am returning you to Cassylia for trial and sentencing."

"Ah, yes," Jason sighed. "I'm not surprised to hear that they are still interested in finding me. But I should warn you that there is very little remaining of the three-billion, seventeen-million credits that I won from your casino."

"Cassylia doesn't want the money back," Mikah said as he locked the controls and swung about in his chair. "They don't want you back either. You are their planetary hero now. When you escaped with your ill-gotten gains they realized that they would never see the money again. So they put their propaganda mills to work and you are now known throughout all the adjoining star systems as 'Jason 3-Billion', the living proof of the honesty of their dishonest games, and a lure for all the weak in spirit. You tempt them into gambling for money instead of working honestly for it."

"Pardon me for being thick today," Jason said, shaking his head rapidly to loosen up the stuck synapses. "I'm having a little difficulty in following you. What kind of a policeman are you to arrest me for trial after the charges have been dropped?"

"I'm not a policeman," Mikah said sternly, his long fingers woven tightly together before him, his eyes wide and penetrating. "I'm a believer in Truth—nothing more. The corrupt politicians who control Cassylia have placed you on a pedestal of honor. Honoring you, another—and if possible—a more corrupt man, and behind your image they have waxed fat. But I am going to use the Truth to destroy that image, and when I destroy the image I shall destroy the evil that produced it."

"That's a tall order for one man," Jason said calmly—much calmer than he really felt. "Do you have a cigarette?"

"There is, of course, no tobacco or spirits on this ship. And I am more than one man. I have followers. The Truth Party is already a power to be reckoned with. We have spent much time and energy in tracking you down, but it was worth it. We have followed your dishonest trail into the past, to Mahaut's Planet, to the Nebula Casino on Galipto, through a series of sordid crimes that turns an honest man's stomach. We have warrants for your arrest from each of these places, in some cases even the results of trials and your death sentence."

"I suppose it doesn't bother your sense of legality that those trials were all held in my absence," Jason asked. "Or that I have only fleeced casinos and gamblers—who make their living by fleecing suckers?"

Mikah Samon wiped away this consideration with a wave of his hand. "You have been proven guilty of a number of crimes. No amount of wriggling on the hook can change that. You should be thankful that your revolting record will have a good use in the end. It will be the lever with which we shall topple the grafting government of Cassylia."

"I'm beginning to be sorry that I stopped Kerk and Meta from shooting you," Jason said, shaking his head in wonder. "I have a very strong suspicion that you are going to cause yourself—and a lot of other people—a good deal of trouble before this thing is over. Look at me for instance—" he rattled his wrists in their restraining bands. The servo motors whined a bit as the detector unit came to life and tightened the grasp of the cuffs, limiting his movement. "A little while ago I was enjoying my health and freedom and I threw it all away on the impulse to save your life. I'm going to have to learn to fight those impulses."

"If that is supposed to be a plea for mercy, it is sickening," Mikah said. "I have never taken favors nor do I owe anything to men of your type. Nor will I ever."

"*Ever* like *never* is a long time," Jason said very quietly. "I wish I had your serenity of mind about the sure order of things."

"Your remark shows that there might be hope for you yet. You might be able to recognise the Truth before you die. I will help you, talk to you and explain."

"Better the execution," Jason choked.

II

"Are you going to feed me by hand—or unlock my wrists while I eat?" Jason asked. Mikah stood over him with the tray, undecided. Jason gave a light verbal prod, very gently, because whatever else he was, Mikah was not stupid. "I would prefer you to feed me of course, you'd make an excellent body servant."

"You are capable of eating by yourself," Mikah responded instantly, sliding the tray into the slots of Jason's chair. "But you will have to do it with only one hand. If you were freed you would only cause trouble." He touched the control on the back of the chair and the right wrist lock snapped open. Jason stretched his cramped fingers and picked up the fork.

While he ate Jason's eyes were busy. Not obviously, since a gambler's attention is never obvious, but many things can be seen if you keep your eyes open and your attention apparently elsewhere. A sudden glimpse of someone's cards, the slight change of expression that reveals a player's strength. Item by item his seemingly random gaze touched the items in the cabin: control console, screens, computer, chart screen, jump control chart case, bookshelf.

Everything was observed, remembered and considered. Some combination of them would fit into the plan.

So far all he had was the beginning and the end of an idea. Beginning: He was a prisoner in this ship, on his way back to Cassylia. End: He was not going to remain a prisoner—nor return to Cassylia. Now all that was missing was the vital middle. It looked impossible at the moment, but Jason never considered that it couldn't be done. He operated on the principle that you made your own luck. You kept your eyes open as things evolved and at the right moment you acted. If you acted fast enough, that was good luck. If you worried over the possibilities until the moment had passed, that was bad luck.

He pushed the empty plate away and stirred sugar into his cup. Mikah had eaten sparingly and was now starting on his second cup of tea. His eyes were fixed, unfocused in thought as he drank. He started slightly when Jason called to him.

"Since you don't stock cigarettes on this ship—how about letting me smoke my own? You'll have to dig them out for me since I can't reach the pocket while I'm chained to this chair."

"I cannot help you," Mikah said, unmoving. "Tobacco is an irritant, a drug and a carcinogen. If I gave you a cigarette, I would be giving you cancer."

"Don't be a hypocrite!" Jason snapped, inwardly pleased at the rewarding flush in the other's neck. "They've taken the cancer-producing agents out of tobacco for centuries now. And even if they hadn't—how does that affect this situation. You're taking me to Cassylia to certain death. So why should you concern yourself with the state of my lungs in the future?"

"I hadn't considered it that way. It is just that there are certain rules of life...."

"Are there?" Jason broke in, keeping the initiative and the advantage. "Not as many as you like to think. And you people who are always dreaming up the rules never carry your thinking far enough. You are against drugs. Which drugs? What about the tannic acid in that tea you're drinking? Or the caffeine in it? It's loaded with caffeine—a drug that is both a strong stimulant and a diuretic. That's why you won't find tea in spacesuit canteens. That's a case of a drug forbidden for a good reason. Can you justify your cigarette ban the same way?"

Mikah started to talk, then thought for a moment. "Perhaps you are right. I'm tired, and it is not important." He warily took the cigarette case from Jason's pocket and dropped it onto the tray. Jason didn't attempt to interfere. Mikah poured himself a third cup of tea with a slightly apologetic air.

"You must excuse me, Jason, for attempting to make you conform to my own standards. When you are in pursuit of the big Truths, you sometimes let the little Truths slip. I'm not intolerant, but I do tend to expect everyone else to live up to certain criteria I have set for myself. Humility is something we should never forget and I thank you for reminding me of it. The search for Truth is hard."

"There is no Truth," Jason told him, the anger and insult gone now from his voice since he wanted to keep his captor involved in the conversation. Involved enough to forget about the free wrist for a while. He raised the cup to his lips and let the tea touch his lips without drinking any. The half-full cup supplied an unconsidered reason for his free hand.

"No Truth?" Mikah weighed the thought. "You can't possibly mean that. The galaxy is filled with Truth, it's the touchstone of Life itself. It's the thing that separates Mankind from the animals."

"There is no Truth, no Life, no Mankind. At least not the way you spell them—with capital letters. They don't exist."

Mikah's taut skin contracted into a furrow of concentration. "You'll have to explain yourself," he said. "You're not being clear."

"I'm afraid it's you who aren't being clear. You're making a reality where none exists. Truth—with a small T is a description, a relationship. A way to describe a statement. A semantic tool. But capital *T* Truth is an imaginary word, a noise with no meaning. It pretends to be a noun but it has no referent. It stands for nothing. It means nothing. When you say 'I believe in Truth' you are really saying 'I believe in nothing'."

"You're wrong, you're wrong," Mikah said, leaning forward, stabbing with his finger. "Truth is a philosophical abstraction, one of the tools that mankind's mind has used to raise it above the beasts—the proof that we are not beasts ourselves, but a higher order of creation. Beasts can be true—but they cannot know Truth. Beasts can see, but they cannot see Beauty."

***

"Arrgh!" Jason growled. "It's impossible to talk to you, much less enjoy any comprehensible exchange of ideas. We aren't even speaking the same language. Aside from who is right and who is wrong, for the moment, we should go back to basics and at least agree on the meaning of the terms that we are using. To begin with—can you define the difference between *ethics* and *ethos*?"

"Of course," Mikah snapped, a glint of pleasure in his eyes at the thought of a good rousing round of hair-splitting. "Ethics is the discipline dealing with what it good or bad, or right or wrong—or with moral duty and obligation. Ethos means the guiding beliefs, standards or ideals that characterize a group or community."

"Very good, I can see that you have been spending the long spaceship-nights with your nose buried in the books. Now make sure the difference between those two terms is very clear, because it is the heart of the little communications problem we have here. Ethos is inextricably linked with a single society and cannot be separated from it, or it loses all meaning. Do you agree?"

"Well...."

"Come, come—you *have* to agree on the terms of your own definition. The ethos of a group is just a catch-all term for the ways in which the members of a group rub against each other. Right?"

16

Mikah reluctantly produced a nod of acquiescence.

"Now that we agree about that we can push on one step further. Ethics, again by your definition, must deal with any number of societies or groups. If there are any absolute laws of ethics, they must be so inclusive that they can be applied to *any* society. A law of ethics must be as universal of application as is the law of gravity."

"I don't follow you...?"

"I didn't think you would when I got to this point. You people who prattle about your Universal Laws never really consider the exact meaning of the term. My knowledge of the history of science is very vague, but I'm willing to bet that the first Law of Gravity ever dreamed up stated that things fell at such and such a speed, and accelerated at such and such a rate. That's not a law, but an observation that isn't even complete until you add 'on this planet.' On a planet with a different mass there will be a different observation. The law of gravity is the formula

$$F = \frac{mM}{d^{\wedge}2}$$

and this can be used to compute the force of gravity between any two bodies anywhere. This is a way of expressing fundamental and unalterable principles that apply in all circumstances. If you are going to have any real ethical laws they will have to have this same universality. They will have to work on Cassylia or Pyrrus, or on any planet or in any society you can find. Which brings us back to you. What you so grandly call—with capital letters and a flourish of trumpets—'Laws of Ethics' aren't laws at all, but are simple little chunks of tribal ethos, aboriginal observations made by a gang of desert sheepherders to keep order in the house—or tent. These rules aren't capable of any universal application, even you must see that. Just think of the different planets that you have been on and the number of weird and wonderful ways people have of reacting to each other—then try and visualize ten rules of conduct that would be applicable in all these societies. An impossible task. Yet I'll bet that you have ten rules you want me to obey, and if one of them is wasted on an injunction against saying prayers to carved idols I can imagine just how universal the other nine are. You aren't being ethical if you try to apply them wherever you go—you're just finding a particularly fancy way to commit suicide!"

"You are being insulting!"

"I hope so. If I can't reach you in any other way, perhaps insult will jar you out of your state of moral smugness. How dare you even consider having me tried for stealing money from the Cassylia casino when all I was doing was conforming to their own code of ethics! They run crooked gambling games, so the law under their local ethos must be that crooked gambling is the norm. So I cheated them, conforming to their norm. If they have also passed a law that says cheating at gambling is illegal, the *law* is unethical, not the cheating. If you are bringing me back to be tried by that law you are unethical, and I am the helpless victim of an evil man."

"Limb of Satan!" Mikah shouted, leaping to his feet and pacing back and forth before Jason, clasping and unclasping his hands with agitation. "You seek to confuse me with your semantics and so-called ethics that are simply opportunism and greed. There is a Higher Law that cannot be argued—"

"That is an impossible statement—and I can prove it." Jason pointed at the books on the wall. "I can prove it with your own books, some of that light reading on the shelf there. Not the Aquinas—too thick. But the little volume with *Lull* on the spine. Is that Ramon Lull's 'The Booke of the Ordre of Chyualry'?"

Mikah's eyes widened. "You know the book? You're acquainted with Lull's writing?"

"Of course," Jason said, with an offhandedness he did not feel, since this was the only book in the collection he could remember reading, the odd title had stuck in his head. "Now let me see it and I shall prove to you what I mean." There was no way to tell from the unchanged naturalness of his words that this was the moment he had been working carefully towards. He sipped the tea. None of his tenseness showing.

Mikah Samon got the book and handed it to him.

Jason flipped through the pages while he talked. "Yes ... yes, this is perfect. An almost ideal example of your kind of thinking. Do you like to read Lull?"

"Inspirational!" Mikah answered, his eyes shining. "There is beauty in every line and Truths that we have forgotten in the rush of modern life. A reconciliation and proof of the interrelationship between the Mystical and the Concrete. By manipulation of symbols he explains everything by absolute logic."

"He proves nothing about nothing," Jason said emphatically. "He plays word games. He takes a word, gives it an abstract and unreal value, then proves this value by relating it to other words with the same sort of nebulous antecedents. His facts aren't facts—just meaningless sounds. This is the key point, where your universe and mine differ. You live in this world of meaningless facts that have no existence. My world contains facts that can be weighed, tested, proven related to other facts in a logical manner. My facts are unshakeable and unarguable. They exist."

"Show me one of your unshakeable facts," Mikah said, his voice calmer now than Jason's.

"Over there," Jason said. "The large green book over the console. It contains facts that even you will agree are true—I'll eat every page if you don't. Hand it to me." He sounded angry, making overly bold statements and Mikah fell right into the trap. He handed the volume to Jason, using both hands since it was very thick, metal bound and heavy.

"Now listen closely and try and understand, even if it is difficult for you," Jason said, opening the book. Mikah smiled wryly at this

assumption of his ignorance. "This is a stellar ephemeris, just as packed with facts as an egg is with meat. In some ways it is a history of mankind. Now look at the jump screen there on the control console and you will see what I mean. Do you see the horizontal green line? Well, that's our course."

"Since this is my ship and I'm flying it I'm aware of that," Mikah said. "Get on with your proof."

"Bear with me," Jason told him. "I'll try and keep it simple. Now the red dot on the green line is our ship's position. The number above the screen our next navigational point, the spot where a star's gravitational field it strong enough to be detected in jump space. The number is the star's code listing. DB89-046-229. I'll look it up in the book"—he quickly flipped the pages—"and find its listing. No name. A row of code symbols though that tell a lot about it. This little symbol means that there is a planet or planets suitable for man to live on. Doesn't say if any people are there though."

"Where does this all lead to?" Mikah interrupted.

"Patience—you'll see in a moment. Now look, at the screen. The green dot approaching on the course line is the PMP. Point of Maximum Proximity. When the red dot and green dot coincide...."

"Give me that book," Mikah ordered, stepping forward. Aware suddenly that something was wrong. He was just an instant too late.

"Here's your proof," Jason said, and hurled the heavy book through the jump screen into the delicate circuits behind. Before it hit he had thrown the second book. There was a tinkling crash, a flare of light and the crackle of shorted circuits.

The floor gave a tremendous heave as the relays snapped open, dropping the ship through into normal space.

Mikah grunted in pain, clubbed to the floor by the suddenness of the transition. Locked into the chair, Jason fought the heaving of his stomach and the blackness before his eyes. As Mikah dragged himself to his feet, Jason took careful aim and sent the tray and dishes hurtling into the smoking ruin of the jump computer.

"There's your fact," he said in cheerful triumph. "Your incontrovertible, gold-plated, uranium-cored fact.

"We're not going to Cassylia any more!"

III

"You've killed us both," Mikah said with his face strained and white but his voice under control.

"Not quite," Jason told him cheerily. "But I have killed the jump control so we can't get to another star. However there's nothing wrong with our space drive, so we can make a landing on one of the planets—you saw for yourself that there is at least one suitable for habitation."

"Where I will fix the jump drive and continue the voyage to Cassylia. You will have gained nothing."

"Perhaps," Jason answered in his most noncommittal voice, since he did not have the slightest intention of continuing the trip, no matter what Mikah Samon thought.

His captor had reached the same conclusion. "Put your hand back on the chair arm," he ordered, and locked the cuff into place again. He stumbled as the drive started and the ship changed direction. "What was that?" he asked.

"Emergency control. The ship's computer knows that something drastic is wrong, so it has taken over. You can override it with the manuals, but don't bother yet. The ship can do a better job than either of us with its senses and stored data. It will find the planet we're looking for, plot a course and get us there with the most economy of time and fuel. When we get into the atmosphere you can take over and look for a spot to set down."

"I don't believe a word you say now," Mikah said grimly. "I'm going to take control and get a call out on the emergency band. Someone will hear it." As he started forward the ship lurched again and all the lights went out. In the darkness flames could be seen flickering inside the controls. There was a hiss of foam and they vanished. With a weak flicker the emergency lighting circuit came on.

"Shouldn't have thrown the Ramon Lull book," Jason said. "The ship can't stomach it any more than I could."

"You are irreverent and profane," Mikah said through his clenched teeth, as he went to the controls. "You attempt to kill us both. You have no respect for your own life or mine. You're a man who deserves the worst punishment the law allows."

"I'm a gambler," Jason laughed. "Not at all as bad as you say. I take chances—but I only take them when the odds are right. You were carrying me back to certain death. The worst my wrecking the controls can do is administer the same end. So I took a chance. There is a bigger risk factor for you of course, but I'm afraid I didn't take that into consideration. After all, this entire affair is your idea. You'll just have to take the consequences of your own actions and not scold me for them."

"You're perfectly right," Mikah said quietly. "I should have been more alert. Now will you tell me what to do to save *both* our lives. None of the controls work."

"None! Did you try the emergency override? The big red switch under the safety housing."

"I did. It is dead, too."

Jason slumped back into the seat. It was a moment before he could speak. "Read one of your books, Mikah," he said at last. "Seek consolation in your philosophy. There's nothing we can do. It's all up to the computer now, and whatever is left of the circuits."

"Can't we help—repair anything?"

"Are you a ship technician? I'm not. We would probably do more harm than good."

***

It took two ship-days of very erratic flight to reach the planet. A haze of clouds obscured the atmosphere. They approached from the night side and no details were visible. Or lights.

"If there were cities we should see their lights—shouldn't we?" Mikah asked.

"Not necessarily. Could be storms. Could be enclosed cities. Could be only ocean in this hemisphere."

"Or it could be that there are no people down there. Even if the ship should get us down safely—what will it matter? We will be trapped for the rest of our lives on this lost planet at the end of the universe."

"Don't be so cheerful," Jason interrupted. "How about taking off these cuffs while we go down. It will probably be a rough landing and I'd like to have some kind of a chance."

Mikah frowned at him. "Will you give me your word of honor that you won't try to escape during the landing?"

"No. And if I gave it—would you believe it? If you let me go, you take your chances. Let neither of us think it will be any different."

"I have my duty to do," Mikah said. Jason remained locked in the chair.

They were in the atmosphere, the gentle sighing against the hull quickly climbed the scale to a shrill scream. The drive cut out and they were in free fall. Air friction heated the outer hull white-hot and the interior temperature quickly rose in spite of the cooling unit.

"What's happening?" Mikah asked. "You seem to know more about this. Are we through—going to crash?"

23

"Maybe. Could be only one of two things. Either the whole works has folded up—in which case we are going to be scattered in very small pieces all over the landscape, or the computer is saving itself for one last effort. I hope that's it. They build computers smart these days, all sort of problem-solving circuits. The hull and engines are in good shape—but the controls spotty and unreliable. In a case like this a good human pilot would let the ship drop as far and fast as it could before switching on the drive. Then turn it on full—thirteen gees or more, whatever he figured the passengers could take on the couches. The hull would take a beating, but who cares. The control circuits would be used the shortest amount of time in the simplest manner."

"Do you think that's what is happening?" Mikah asked, getting into his acceleration chair.

"That's what I *hope* is happening. Going to unlock the cuffs before you go to bed? It could be a bad landing and we might want to go places in a hurry."

Mikah considered, then took out his gun. "I'll unlock you, but I intend to shoot if you try anything. Once we are down you will be locked in again."

"Thanks for small blessings," Jason said, rubbing his wrists.

Deceleration jumped on them, kicked the air from their lungs in uncontrollable gasps, sank them deep into the yielding couches. Mikah's gun was pressed into his chest, too heavy to lift. It made no difference, Jason could not stand nor move. He hovered on the border of consciousness, his vision flickering behind a black and red haze.

Just as suddenly the pressure was gone.

They were still falling.

The drive groaned in the stern of the ship and relays chattered. But it didn't start again. The two men stared at each other, unmoving, for the unmeasurable unit of time that the ship fell.

As the ship dropped it turned and hit at an angle. The end came for Jason in an engulfing wave of thunder, shock and pain. Sudden impact pushed him against the restraining straps, burst them with the inertia of his body, hurled him across the control room. His last conscious thought was to protect his head. He was lifting his arm when he struck the wall.

****

There is a cold that is so chilling it is a pain not a temperature. Cold that slices into the flesh before it numbs and kills.

Jason came to with the sound of his own voice crying hoarsely. The cold was so great it filled the universe. Cold water he realized as he coughed it from his mouth and nose. Something was around him and it took an effort to recognize it as Mikah's arm; he was holding Jason's face above the surface while he swam. A receding blackness in the water could only have been the ship, giving off bubbles and groans as it died. The cold water didn't hurt now and Jason was just relaxing when he felt something solid under his feet.

"Stand up and walk, curse you," Mikah gasped hoarsely. "I can't ... carry you ... can't carry myself...."

They floundered out of the water, side by side, four-legged crawling beasts that could not stand erect. Everything had an unreality to it and Jason found it hard to think. He should not stop, that he was sure of, but what else could he do? There was a flickering in the darkness, a wavering light coming towards them. Jason could say nothing, but he heard Mikah cry out for help.

Nearer came the light, some kind of a flare or torch, held high. Mikah pulled to his feet as the flame approached.

It was a nightmare. It wasn't a man but a thing that held the flare. A thing of angles, sharp corners, fang-faced and horrible. It had a clubbed extremity it used to strike down Mikah. The tall man fell wordlessly and the creature turned towards Jason. He had no strength to fight with, though he struggled to climb to his feet. His fingers scratched at the frosted sand, but he could not rise, and exhausted with this last effort he fell forward face down. Unconsciousness pulled at his brain but he would not submit. The flickering torchlight came closer and the scuffle of heavy feet in the sand; he could not have this horror behind him. With the last of his strength he levered himself over and lay on his back, staring up at the thing that stood over him, with the darkness of exhaustion filming his eyes.

IV

It did not kill him at once, but stood staring down at him, and as the slow seconds ticked by and Jason was still alive he forced himself to consider this menace that appeared from the blackness.

"*K'e vi stas el...?*" the creature said, and for the first time Jason realized it was human. The meaning of the question picked at the edge of his exhausted brain, he felt he could almost understand it, though he had never heard the language before. He tried to answer but there was only a hoarse gargle from his throat.

"*Ven k'n torcoy—r'pidu!*"

More lights sprang from the darkness inland and with them the sound of running feet. As they came closer Jason had a clearer look at the man above him and could understand why he had mistaken him for some inhuman creature. His limbs were completely wrapped in lengths of stained leather, his chest and body protected by thick and overlapping leather plates covered with blood-red designs. Over his head was fitted the cochlea shaped shell of some animal, spiraling to a point in front: two small openings had been drilled in it for eye holes. Great, finger-long teeth had been set in the lower edge of the shell to heighten the already fearsome appearance. The only thing at all human about the creature was the matted and filthy beard that trickled out of the shell below the teeth. There were too many other details for Jason to absorb so suddenly; something bulky slung behind one shoulder, dark objects at the waist, a heavy club reached and

26

prodded Jason in the ribs, but he was too close to unconsciousness to resist.

A guttural command halted the torch-bearers a full five meters from the spot where Jason lay. He wondered vaguely why the armored man had not let them approach closer since the light from their torches barely reached this far: everything on this planet seemed inexplicable. For a few moments Jason must have lost consciousness because when he looked again the torch was stuck in the sand at his side and the armored man had one of Jason's boots off and was pulling at the other. Jason could only writhe feebly but not prevent the theft, for some reason he could not force his body to follow his will. His sense of time seemed to have altered as well and though every second dragged heavily by events occurred with startling rapidity.

The boots were gone now and the man fumbled at Jason's clothes, stopping every few seconds to glance up at the row of torch-bearers. The magnetic seals were alien to him, the sharp teeth sewn into the leather over his knuckles dug into Jason's flesh as he struggled to open the seals or to tear the resistant metalcloth. He was growling with impatience when he accidentally touched the release button on the medikit and it dropped into his hand. The shining gadget seemed to please him, but when one of the sharp needles slipped through his thick hand-coverings and stabbed him he howled with rage, throwing the machine down, and grinding it into a splintered ruin in the sand. The loss of this irreplaceable device goaded Jason into motion, he sat up and was trying to reach the medikit when unconsciousness surged over him.

***

Sometime before dawn the pain in his head drove him reluctantly back to awareness. There were some foul-smelling hides draped over him that retained a little of his body heat. He pulled away the stifling fold that covered his face and stared up at the stars, cold points of light that glittered in the frigid night. The air was a stimulant and he sucked deep gasps of it that burned his throat but seemed to clear his thoughts. For the first time he realized that his disorientation had been caused by that crack on the head he had received when the ship crashed; his exploring fingers found a swollen rawness on his skull. He must have a brain concussion, that would explain his earlier inability to move or think straight. The cold air was numbing his face and he willingly pulled the hairy skin back over his head.

He wondered what had happened to Mikah Samon after the local thug in the horror outfit had bashed him with the club. This was a messy and unexpected end for the man after he had managed to survive the crash of the ship. Jason had no special affection for the under-nourished zealot, but he did owe him a life. Mikah had saved him after the crash, only to be murdered himself by this local assassin. Jason made a mental note to kill the man just as soon as he was physically up to it, at the same time he was a little astonished at his reflexive acceptance of the need for this blood-thirsty atonement of a life for a life. Apparently his long stay on Pyrrus had trodden down his normal dislike for killing except in self-defense and from what he had seen so far of this world the Pyrran training would certainly be most useful. The sky showed gray through a tear in the hide and he pushed it back to look at the dawn.

Mikah Samon lay next to him his head projecting from a covering fur. He hair was matted and caked with dark blood, but he was still breathing.

"Harder to kill than I thought," Jason grunted as he levered himself painfully up onto one elbow and took a good look at this world where his spaceship sabotage had landed them.

It was a grim desert, lumped with huddled bodies like the aftermath of a battle at world's-end. A few of them were stumbling to their feet, holding their skins around them, the only signs of life in that immense waste of gritty sand. On one side a ridge of dunes cut off sight of the sea, but he could hear the dull boom of waves on the shore. White frost rimed the ground and the chill wind made his eyes blink and water. On the top of the dunes a remembered figure suddenly appeared, the armored man, doing something with what appeared to be lengths of rope; there was metallic tinkling, suddenly cut off. Mikah Samon groaned and stirred.

"How do you feel," Jason asked. "Those are two of the finest blood-shot eyeballs I have ever seen."

"Where am I?"

"Now that is a bright and original question—I didn't pick you for the type who watched historical spaceopera on the TV. I have no idea where we are—but I can give you a brief synopsis of how we arrived here, if you are up to it."

"I remember we swam ashore, then something evil came from the darkness, like a demon from hell. We fought...."

"And he bashed in your head, one quick blow and that was about all the fight there was. I had a better look at your demon, though I was in no better condition to fight him than you were. He's a man dressed in a weird outfit out of an addict's nightmare and appears to be the boss of this crew of rugged campers. Other than that I have little idea of what is going on—except that he stole my boots and I'm going to get then back if I have to kill him for them."

"Do not lust after material things," Mikah intoned seriously. "And do not talk of killing a man for material gain. You are evil, Jason, and.... My boots are gone—and my clothes, too!"

Mikah had thrown back his covering skins and made this startling discovery. "Belial!" he roared. "Asmodeus, Abaddon, Apollyon and Baal-zebub!"

"Very nice," Jason said admiringly, "you really have been studying up on your demonology. Were you just listing them—or calling on them for aid?"

"Silence, blasphemer! I have been robbed!" He rose to his feet and the wind whistling around his almost-bare body quickly gave his skin a light touch of blue. "I am going to find the evil creature that did this and force him to return what is mine."

Mikah turned to leave but Jason reached out and grabbed his ankle with a wrestling grip, twisted it and brought the man thudding to the ground. The fall dazed him and Jason pulled the skins back over the raw-boned form.

"We're even," Jason said. "You saved my life last night, just now I saved yours. You're bare-handed and wounded—while the old man of the mountain up there is a walking armory, and anyone with the personality to wear that kind of an outfit will kill you as easily as he picks his teeth. So take it easy and try to avoid trouble. There's a way out of this mess—there's a way out of *every* mess if you look for it—and I'm going to find it. In fact I'm going to take a walk right now and start my research. Agreed?"

A groan was his only answer since Mikah was unconscious again, fresh blood seeping from his injured scalp. Jason stood and wrapped his hides about his body as some protection from the wind, tying the loose ends together. Then he kicked through the sand until he found a smooth rock that would fit inside his fist with just the end protruding, and thus armed made his way out through the stirring forms of the sleepers.

***

Mikah was conscious again when Jason returned, and the sun was well above the horizon. The people were all awake now, a shuffling, scratching herd of about thirty men, women and children. They were identical in their filth and crude skin wrappings, milling about with a random motion or sitting blankly on the ground. They showed no interest at all in the two strangers. Jason handed a tarred leather cup to Mikah and squatted next to him.

"Drink that. It's water, the only thing that anyone here had to drink. I didn't find any food." He still had the stone in his hand and while he talked he rubbed it on the sand: the end was moist and red and some long hairs were stuck in it.

"I took a good look around this camp, and there's very little more than you can see from here. Just this crowd of broken down types, a few bundles rolled in hide, and some of them are carrying skin water bottles. They have a simple me-stronger pecking order so I pecked a bit and we can drink. Food comes next."

"Who are they? What are we doing?" Mikah asked, mumbling a little, obviously still suffering the after-effects of the blow. Jason looked at the contused skull, and decided not to touch it. The wound had bled freely and clotted. Washing it off with the highly dubious water would accomplish little and might add infection to their other troubles.

"I'm only sure of one thing," Jason said. "They're slaves. I don't know why they are here, what they are doing or where they are going, but their status is painfully clear—ours, too. Old Nasty up there on the hill is the boss. The rest of us are slaves."

"Slaves!" Mikah snorted, the word penetrating through the pain in his head. "It is abominable. The slaves must be freed."

"No lectures please, and try to be realistic—even if it hurts. There are only two slaves that need freeing here, you and I. These people seem nicely adjusted to the *status quo* and I see no reason to change it. I'm not starting any abolitionist campaigns until I can see my way clearly out of this mess, and I probably won't start any then either. This planet has been going on a long time without me, and will probably keep rolling along once I'm gone."

"Coward! You must fight for the Truth and the Truth will make you free."

"I can hear those capital letters again," Jason groaned. "The only thing right now that is going to make me free is me. Which may be bad poetry, but is still the truth. The situation here is rough but not unbeatable—so listen and learn. The boss, his name is Ch'aka in case you care, seems to have gone off on a hunt of some kind. He's not far away and will be back soon, so I'll try and give you the entire setup quickly.

"I thought I recognized the language, and I was right. It's a corrupt form of Esperanto, the language all the Terido worlds speak. This altered language plus the fact that these people live about one step above the stone-age culture is pretty sure evidence that they are cut off from any contact with the rest of the galaxy, though I hope not. There may be a trading base somewhere on the planet, and if there is we'll find it later. We have enough other things to worry about right now, but at least we can speak the language. These people have contracted and lost a lot of sounds and even introduced a glottal stop, something that *no* language needs, but with a little effort the meaning can still be made out."

"I do not speak Esperanto."

"Then learn it. It's easy enough even in this jumbled form. And shut up and listen. These locals are born and bred slaves and it is all they know. There is a little squabbling in the ranks with the bigger ones pushing the work on the weak ones when Ch'aka isn't looking, but I have that situation well in hand. Ch'aka is our big problem, and we have to find out a lot more things before we can tackle him. He is boss, fighter, father, provider and destiny for this mob, and he seems to know his job. So try to be a good slave for a while...."

"Slave! I?" Mikah arched his back and tried to rise. Jason pushed him back to the ground—harder than was necessary.

"Yes, you—and me, too. That is the only way we are going to survive in this arrangement. Do what everyone else does, obey orders, and you stand a good chance of staying alive until we can find a way out of this tangle."

***

Mikah's answer was drowned out in a roar from the dunes as Ch'aka returned. The slaves climbed quickly to their feet, grabbing up their bundles, and began to form a single widespaced line. Jason helped Mikah to stand and wrap strips of skin around his feet then supported most of his weight as they stumbled to a place in the open formation. Once they were all in position Ch'aka kicked the nearest one and they began walking slowly forward looking carefully at the ground as they went. Jason had no idea of the significance of the action, but as long as he and Mikah weren't bothered it didn't matter: he had enough work cut out for him just to keep the wounded man on his feet. Somehow Mikah managed to dredge up enough strength to keep going.

One of the slaves pointed down and shouted and the line stopped. He was too far away for Jason to make out the cause of the excitement, but the man bent over and scratched a hole with a short length of pointed wood. In a few seconds he dug up something round and not quite the size of his hand. He raised it over his head and brought the thing to Ch'aka at a shambling run. The slavemaster took it and bit off a chunk, and when the man who had found it turned away he gave him a lusty kick. The line moved forward again.

Two more of the mysterious objects were found, both of which Ch'aka ate as well. Only when his immediate hunger was satisfied did he make any attempt to be the good provider. When the next one was found he called over a slave and threw the object into a crudely woven basket he was carrying on his back. After this the basket-toting slave walked directly in front of Ch'aka who was carefully watchful that every one of the things that was dug up went into the basket. Jason wondered what they were—and they were edible, too, an angry rumbling in his stomach reminded him.

The slave next in line to Jason shouted and pointed to the sand. Jason let Mikah sink to a sitting position when they stopped and watched with interest as the slave attacked the ground with his piece of wood, scratching around a tiny sprig of green that projected from the desert sand. His burrowings uncovered a wrinkled gray object from which the green leaves were growing, a root or tuber of some kind. It appeared as edible as a piece of stone to Jason, but obviously not to the slave who drooled heavily and actually had the temerity to sniff the root. Ch'aka howled with anger at this and when the slave had dropped the root into the basket with the others he received a kick so strong that he had to limp back painfully to his position in the line.

Soon after this Ch'aka called a halt and the tattered slaves huddled around while he poked through the basket. He called them over one at a time and gave them one or more of the roots according to some merit system of his own. The basket was almost empty when he poked his club at Jason.

"K'e nam h'vas vi?" he asked.

"Mia namo estas Jason, mia amiko estas Mikah."

Jason answered in correct Esperanto that Ch'aka seemed to understand well enough, because he grunted and dug through the contents of the basket. His masked face stared at them and Jason could feel the impact of the unseen watching eyes. The club pointed again.

"Where you come from? That you ship that burn, sink?"

"That was our ship. We come from far away."

"From other side of ocean?" This was apparently the largest distance the slaver could imagine.

"From the other side of the ocean, correct." Jason was in no mood to deliver a lecture on astronomy. "When do we eat?"

"You a rich man in your country, got a ship, got shoes. Now I got your shoes. You a slave here. My slave. You both my slaves."

"I'm your slave, I'm your slave," Jason said resignedly. "But even slaves have to eat. Where's the food?"

Ch'aka grubbed around in the basket until he found a tiny and withered root which he broke in half and threw onto the sand in front of Jason.

"Work hard you get more."

Jason picked up the pieces and brushed away as much of the dirt as he could. He handed one to Mikah and took a tentative bite out of the other one: it was gritty with sand and tasted like slightly rancid wax. It took a distinct effort to eat the repulsive thing but he did.

Without a doubt it was food, no matter how unwholesome, and would do until something better came along.

"What did you talk about?" Mikah asked, grinding his own portion between his teeth.

"Just swapping lies. He thinks we're his slaves and I agreed. But it's just temporary—" Jason added as anger colored Mikah's face and he started to climb to his feet. Jason pulled him back down. "This is a strange planet, you're injured, we have no food or water, and no idea at all how to survive in this place. The only thing we can do to stay alive is to go along with what Old Ugly there says. If he wants to call us slaves, fine—we're slaves."

"Better to die free than to live in chains!"

"Will you stop the nonsense. Better to live in chains and learn how to get rid of them. That way you end up alive-free rather than dead-free, a much more attractive state. Now shut up and eat. We can't do anything until you are out of the walking wounded class."

***

For the rest of the day the line of walkers plodded across the sand and in addition to helping Mikah, Jason found two of the *krenoj*, the edible roots. They stopped before dusk and dropped gratefully to the sand. When the food was divided they received a slightly larger portion, as evidence perhaps of Jason's attention to the work. Both men were exhausted and fell asleep as soon as it was dark.

During the following morning they had their first break from the walking routine. Their foodsearching always paralleled the unseen sea, and one slave walked the crest of the dunes that hid the water from sight. He must have seen something of interest because he leaped down from the mound and waved both arms wildly. Ch'aka ran heavily to the dunes and talked with the scout, then booted the man from his presence.

Jason watched with growing interest as he unwrapped the bulky package slung from his back and disclosed an efficient looking

35

crossbow, cocking it by winding on a built-in crank. This complicated and deadly piece of machinery seemed very much out of place with the primitive slave-holding society, and Jason wished that he could get a better look at the device. Ch'aka fumbled a quarrel from another pouch and fitted it to the bow. The slaves sat silently on the sand while their master stalked along the base of the dunes, then wormed his way over them and out of sight, creeping silently on his stomach. A few minutes later there was a scream of pain from behind the dunes and all the slaves jumped to their feet and raced to see. Jason left Mikah where he lay and was in the first rank of observers that broke over the hillocks and onto the shore.

They stopped at the usual distance and shouted compliments about the quality of the shot and what a mighty hunter Ch'aka was. Jason had to admit there was a certain truth in the claims. A large, furred amphibian lay at the water's edge, the fletched end of the crossbow bolt projecting from its thick neck and a thin stream of blood running down to mix with the surging waves.

"Meat! Meat today!"

"Ch'aka kills the *rosmaro*! Ch'aka is wonderful!"

"Hail, Ch'aka, great provider," Jason shouted to get into the swing of things. "When do we eat?"

The master ignored his slaves, sitting heavily on the dune until he regained his breath after the stalk. Then after cocking the crossbow again he stalked over to the beast and with his knife cut out the quarrel, notching it against the bowstring still dripping with blood.

"Get wood for fire," he commanded. "You, Opisweni, you use the knife."

Shuffling backwards Ch'aka sat down on a hillock and pointed the crossbow at the slave who approached the kill. Ch'aka had left his knife in the animal and Opisweni pulled it free and began to methodically flay and butcher the beast. All the time he worked he carefully kept his back turned to Ch'aka and the aimed bow.

"A trusting soul, our slave-driver," Jason mumbled to himself as he joined the others in searching the shore for driftwood. Ch'aka had all the weapons as well as a constant fear of assassination. If Opisweni tried to use the knife for anything other than the intended piece of work, he would get the crossbow quarrel in the back of his head. Very efficient.

Enough driftwood was found to make a sizable fire, and when Jason returned with his contribution the *rosmaro* had been hacked into large chunks. Ch'aka kicked his slaves away from the heap of wood and produced a small device from another of his sacks. Interested, Jason pushed as close as he dared, into the front rank of the watching circle. Though he had never seen one of them before, the operation of the firemaker was obvious to him. A spring-loaded arm drove a fragment of stone against a piece of steel, sparks flew out and were caught in a cup of tinder, where Ch'aka blew on them until they burst into flame.

Where had the firelighter and the crossbow come from? They were evidence of a higher level of culture than that possessed by these slave-holding nomads. This was the first bit of evidence that Jason had seen that there might be more to the cultural life of this planet than they had seen since their landing. Later, while they were gorging themselves on the seared meat, he drew Mikah aside and pointed this out.

"There's hope yet. These illiterate thugs never manufactured that crossbow or firelighter. We must find out where they came from and see about getting there ourselves. I had a quick look at the quarrel when Ch'aka pulled it out, and I'll swear that it was turned from steel."

"This has significance?" Mikah asked, puzzled.

"It means an industrial society, and possible interstellar contact."

"Then we must ask Ch'aka where he obtained them and leave at once. There will be authorities, we will contact them, explain the situation, obtain transportation to Cassylia. I will not place you under arrest again until that time."

Ijale

"How considerate of you," Jason said, lifting one eyebrow. Mikah was absolutely impossible, and Jason probed at his moral armor to see if there were any weak spots. "Won't you feel guilty about bringing me back to get killed? After all we are companions in trouble—and I did save your life."

"I will grieve, Jason. I can see that though you are evil you are not completely evil, and given the right training could be fitted for a useful place in society. But my personal grief must not be allowed to alter events: you forget that you committed a crime and must pay the penalty."

Ch'aka belched cavernously inside his shell-helmet and howled at his slaves.

"Enough eating, you pigs. You get fat. Wrap the meat and carry it, we have light yet to look for *krenoj*. Move!"

Once more the line was formed and began its slow pace across the desert. More of the edible roots were found, and once they stopped briefly to fill the water bags at a spring that bubbled up out of the sand. The sun dropped towards the horizon and what little warmth it possessed was absorbed by a bank of clouds. Jason looked around and shivered—then noticed the line of dots moving on the horizon. He nudged Mikah who still leaned heavily on him.

"Looks like company coming. I wonder where they fit into the program?"

Pain had blurred Mikah's attention and he took no notice and, surprisingly enough, neither did any of the other slaves nor Ch'aka. The dots expanded and became another row of marchers, apparently absorbed in the same task as Jason's group. They plodded forward, making a slow examination of the sand, followed behind by the solitary figure of their master. The two lines slowly approached each other, paralleling the shore.

Near the dunes was a crude mound of stones and the line of walking slaves stopped as soon as they reached it, dropping with satisfied grunts onto the sand. The cairn was obviously a border marker and Ch'aka walked to it and rested his foot on one of the stones, watching while the other line of slaves approached. They, too, stopped at the cairn and settled to the ground: both groups stared with dull-eyed lack of interest and only the slave-masters showed any animation. The other master stopped a good ten paces before he reached Ch'aka and waved an evil looking stone hammer over his head.

"Hate you, Ch'aka!" he roared.

"Hate you, Fasimba!" boomed back the answer.

The exchange was as formal as a *pas de deux* and just about as warlike. Both men shook their weapons and shouted a few insults, then settled down to a quiet conversation. Fasimba was garbed in the same type of hideous and fear-inspiring outfit as Ch'aka, differing only in unimportant details. Instead of a conch, his head was encased in the skull of one of the amphibious *rosmaroj*, brightened up with some extra tusks and horns. The differences between the two men were all minor, and mostly a matter of decoration or variation of weapon design. They were obviously slave masters and equals.

"Killed a *rosmaro* today, second time in ten days," Ch'aka said.

"You got a good piece coast. Plenty *rosmaroj*. Where the two slaves you owe me?"

"I owe you two slaves?"

"You owe me two slaves, don't play like stupid. I got the iron arrows for you from the D'zertanoj, one slave you paid with died. You still owe other one."

"I got two slaves for you. I got two slaves more I pulled out of the ocean."

"You got a good piece coast."

Ch'aka walked down his line of slaves until he came to the over-bold one he had half-crippled with a kick the day before. Pulling him to his feet he booted him towards the other mob.

"Here's a good one," he said, delivering the goods with a last parting kick.

"Look skinny. Not too good."

"No, all muscles. Works hard. Doesn't eat much."

"You're a liar!"

"Hate you, Fasimba!"

"Hate you, Ch'aka! Where's the other one?"

"Got a good one. Stranger from the ocean. He can tell you funny stories, work hard."

Jason turned in time to avoid the full force of the kick, but it was still strong enough to knock him sprawling. Before he could get up

Ch'aka had clutched Mikah Samon by the arm and dragged him across the invisible line to the other group of slaves. Fasimba stalked over to examine him, prodding him with a spiked toe.

"Don't look good. Big hole on the head."

"He works hard," Ch'aka said. "Hole almost healed. He very strong."

"You give me new one if he dies?" Fasimba asked doubtfully.

"I'll give you. Hate you, Fasimba!"

"Hate you, Ch'aka."

The slave herds were prodded to their feet and moved back the way they had come, and Jason shouted after Ch'aka.

"Wait! Don't sell my friend. We work better together, you can get rid of someone else...."

The slaves gaped at this sudden outburst and Ch'aka wheeled raising his club.

"You shut up. You're a slave. You tell me once more to do what and I kill you."

Jason shut up since it was very obvious that this was the only thing he could do. He had a few qualms about Mikah's possible fate: if he survived the wound he was certainly not the type to bow to the inevitabilities of slave-holding life. Yet Jason had done his best to save him and that was that. Now Jason would think about Jason for a while.

***

They made a brief march before dark, apparently just until the other slaves were out of sight, then stopped for the night. Jason settled himself into the lee of a mound that broke the force of the wind a bit and unwrapped a piece of scorched meat he had salvaged from the earlier feast. It was tough and oily but far superior to the barely edible *krenoj* that made up the greater part of the native diet. He chewed noisily on the bone and watched while one of the other slaves sidled over towards him.

"Give me some your meat?" the slave asked in a whining voice, and only when she talked did Jason realize that this was a girl; all the slaves were alike in their matted hair and skin wrappings. He ripped off a chunk of meat.

"Here. Sit down and eat it. What's your name?" In exchange for his generosity he intended to get some information from his captive audience.

"Ijale." She tore at the meat, held tightly in one fist, while the index finger of her free hand scratched for enemies in her tangled hair.

"Where do you come from? Did you always live here—like this?" How do you ask a slave if she has always been a slave?

"Not here. I come from Bul'wajo first, then Fasimba, now I belong to Ch'aka."

"What or who is Bul'wajo? Someone like our boss Ch'aka?" She nodded, gnawing at the meat. "And the D'zertanoj that Fasimba gets his arrows from—who are they?"

"You don't know much," she said, finishing the meat and licking the grease from her fingers.

"I know enough to have meat when you don't have any—so don't abuse my hospitality. Who are the D'zertanoj?"

"Everyone knows who they are." She shrugged with incomprehension and looked for a soft spot in the sand to sit down. "They live in the desert. They go around in *caroj*. They stink. They have many nice things. One of them gave me my best thing. If I show it to you, you won't take it?"

"No, I won't touch it. But I would like to see anything they have made. Here, here's some more meat. Now let me see your best thing."

Ijale rooted in her skins for a hidden pocket and dragged out something that she concealed in her clenched fist. She held it out proudly and opened it and there was enough light left for Jason to make out the rough form of a red glass bead.

"Isn't this so very nice?" she asked.

"Very nice," Jason agreed, and for an instant felt a touch of real sorrow when he looked at the pathetic bauble. This girl's ancestors had come to this planet in spaceships with a knowledge of the most advanced sciences. Cut off, their children had degenerated into this, barely conscious slaves, who could pride a worthless piece of glass above all things.

"I like you. I'll show you my best thing again."

"I like you, too. Good night."

V

Ijale stayed near Jason the next day, and took the next station in line when the endless *krenoj* hunt began. Whenever it was possible he questioned her and before noon had extracted all of her meager knowledge of affairs beyond the barren coastal plain where they lived. The ocean was a mystery that produced edible animals, fish and an occasional human corpse. Ships could be seen from time to time offshore but nothing was known about them. On the other flank the territory was bounded by desert even more inhospitable than the one in which they scratched out their existence, a waste of lifeless sand, habitable only by the D'zertanoj and their mysterious *caroj*. These last could be animals—or mechanical transportation of some kind, either was possible from Ijale's vague description. Ocean, coast and desert, these made up all of her world and she could conceive of nothing that might exist beyond.

Jason knew there was more, the crossbow was proof enough of that, and he had every intention of finding out where it came from. In order to do that he was going to have to change his slave status when the proper time came. He was developing a certain facility in dodging Ch'aka's heavy boot, the work was never hard and there was ample food. Being a slave left him with no responsibilities other than obeying orders and he had ample opportunity to discover what he could about this planet, so that when he finally did leave he would be as well prepared as was possible.

Later in the day another column of marching slaves was sighted in the distance, on a course paralleling their own, and Jason expected a repeat performance of the previous day's meeting. He was agreeably surprised that it was not. The sight of the others threw Ch'aka into an immediate rage that sent his slaves rushing for safety in all directions. By leaping into the air, howling with anger and beating his club against his thick leather armor he managed to work himself into quite a state before starting off on a slogging run. Jason, followed close behind him, greatly interested by this new turn of affairs. Ahead of them the other slaves scattered and from their midst burst another armed and armored figure. They churned towards each other at top speed and Jason hoped for a shattering crash when they met. However they slowed before they hit and began circling each other, spitting curses.

"Hate you, M'shika!"

"Hate you, Ch'aka!"

The words were the same, but shouted with fierce meaning, with no touch of formality this time.

"Kill you, M'shika! You coming again on my part of the ground with your carrion-meat slaves!"

"You lie, Ch'aka—this ground mine from way back."

"I kill you way back!"

Ch'aka leaped in as he screamed the words and swung a roundhouse blow with his club that would have broken the other man in two if it had connected. But M'shika was expecting this and fell back, swinging a counter-blow with his own club that Ch'aka easily avoided. There followed a quick exchange of club-work that did little more than fan the air, until suddenly both men were locked together and the fight began in earnest. They rolled together on the ground grunting savagely, tearing at each other. The heavy clubs were of no use this close and were dropped in favor of knives and knees: Jason could understand now why Ch'aka had the long tusks strapped to his kneecaps. It was a no-holds-barred fight and each man was trying as hard as possible to kill his opponent. The leather armor made this difficult and the struggle continued, littering the sand with broken off animal teeth, discarded weapons and other debris. It looked like it would be called a draw when both men separated for a breather, but they dived right back in again.

***

It was Ch'aka who broke the stalemate when he plunged his dagger into the ground and on the next roll caught the handle in his mouth. Holding his opponent's arms in both his hands he plunged his head down and managed to find a weak spot in the other's armor: M'shika howled and pulled free and when he climbed to his feet blood was running down his arm and dripping from his fingertips. Ch'aka jumped after him but the wounded man grabbed up his club in time to ward off the charge. Stumbling backward he managed to pick up most of his discarded weapons with his wounded arm and beat a hasty retreat. Ch'aka ran after him a short way, shouting praise of his own strength and abilities and of his opponent's cowardice. Jason saw a short, sharp horn from some sea animal lying in the churned up sand and quickly picked it up before Ch'aka turned back.

Once his enemy had been chased out of sight Ch'aka carefully searched the battleground and scavenged anything of military value. Though there was still some hours of daylight left he signaled a halt and distributed the evening ration of *krenoj*. Jason sat and chewed his portion reflectively while Ijale leaned against his side, her shoulder moving rhythmically as she scratched some hidden mite. Lice were inescapable, they hid in the crevices of the badly cured hides and emerged with clicking jaws whenever the warmth of

45

human flesh came near. Jason had his quota of the pests and found his scratching keeping time with hers. This syncopation of scratch triggered the anger that had been building within him, slow and unnoticed.

"I'm serving notice," he said, jumping to his feet. "I'm through with this slave business. Which way is the nearest spot in the desert where I can find the D'zertanoj?"

"Over there, a two-day walk. How are you going to kill Ch'aka?"

"I'm not going to kill Ch'aka, I'm just leaving. I've enjoyed his hospitality and his boot long enough and feel like striking out for myself."

"You can't do that," she gasped. "You will be killed."

"Ch'aka can't very well kill me if I'm not here."

"Everybody will kill you. That is the law. Runaway slaves are always killed."

Jason sat down again and cracked another chunk from his *krenoj* and ruminated over it. "You've talked me into staying a while. But I have no particular desire now to kill Ch'aka, even though he did steal my boots. And I don't see how killing him will help me any."

"You are stupid. After you kill Ch'aka you'll be the new Ch'aka. Then you can do what you want."

Of course. Now that he had been told, the social setup appeared obvious. Because he had seen slaves and slave-holders, Jason had held the mistaken notion that they were different classes of society, when in reality there was only one class, what might be called the dog-eat-dog class. He should have been aware of this when he had seen how careful Ch'aka was to never allow anyone within striking distance of him, and how he vanished each night to some hidden spot. This was free enterprise with a vengeance, carried to its absolute extreme with every man out for himself, every other man's hand turned against him, and your station in life determined by the strength of your arm and the speed of your reflexes. Anyone who stayed alone placed himself outside this society and was therefore an enemy of it and sure to be killed on sight. All of which added up to the fact that he had to kill Ch'aka if he wanted to get ahead. He still had no desire to do it, but he had to.

***

That night he watched Ch'aka when he slipped away from the others and Jason made a careful note of the direction that he took. Of course the slave master would circle about before he concealed himself, but with a little luck Jason would find him. And kill him. He had no special love of midnight assassination, and until landing on this planet had always believed that killing a sleeping man was a cowardly way to terminate another's existence. But special conditions demand special solutions, and he was no match for the heavily armored man in open combat, therefore the assassin's knife. Or rather sharpened horn. He managed to doze fitfully until some time after midnight, then slipped silently from under his skin coverings. Silently he skirted the sleepers and crept into the darkness between the dunes.

Finding Ch'aka in the wilderness of the desert night was not easy, yet Jason persisted. He made careful sweeps in wider and wider arcs, working his way out from the sleeping slaves. There were gullies and shadowed ravines and all of them had to be searched with utmost care. The slave master was sleeping in one of them and would be alert for any sound. The fact that he had also made special precautions to guard against assassination was only apparent to Jason after he heard the bell ring. It was a tiny sound, barely detectable, but he froze instantly. There was a thin strand pressing against his arm, and when he drew back carefully the bell sounded again. He cursed silently for his stupidity, only remembering now about the bells he had heard from Ch'aka's sleeping site. The slaver must surround himself every night with a network of string that would sound alarm bells if anyone attempted to approach in the dark. Slowly and soundlessly Jason drew back deeper into the gully.

With a thud of rushing feet Ch'aka appeared, swinging his club around his head, coming directly towards Jason. Jason rolled desperately sideways and the club crashed into the ground, then he was up and running at top speed down the gully. Rocks twisted under his feet and he knew that if he tripped he was dead, yet he had no choice other than flight. The heavily armored Ch'aka could not keep up with him and Jason managed to stay on his feet until the other was left behind. Ch'aka shouted with rage and hurled curses after him, but he could not catch him. Jason, panting for breath, vanished into the darkness and made a slow circle back to the sleeping camp. The noise would have roused them and he stayed away for an estimated hour, shivering in the icy predawn, before he slipped back to his waiting skins. The sky was beginning to gray and he lay awake wondering if he had been recognized: he didn't think he had.

As the red sun climbed over the horizon Ch'aka appeared on top of the dunes, shaking with rage.

"Who did it?" he screamed. "Who came in night." He stalked among them, glaring right and left, and no one stirred except to draw away from his stamping feet. "Who did it?" he shouted again as he came near the spot where Jason lay.

Five slaves pointed silently at Jason.

***

Cursing their betrayal Jason sprang up and ran from the whistling club. He had the sharpened horn in his hand but knew better than to try and stand up to Ch'aka in open combat; there had to be another way. He looked back quickly to see his enemy still following and narrowly missed tripping over the outstretched leg of a slave. They were all against him! They were all against each other and no man was safe from any other man's hand. He ran free of the slaves and scrambled to the top of a shifting dune, pulling himself up the steep slope by clutching at the coarse grass on the summit. He turned at the top and kicked sand into Ch'aka's face, trying to blind him, but had to run when the slaver swung down his crossbow and notched a steel quarrel. Ch'aka chased him again, panting heavily.

Jason was tiring now and he knew this was the best time to launch a counterattack. The slaves were out of sight and it would be a battle only between the two of them. Scrambling up a slope of broken rock he reversed himself suddenly and leaped back down. Ch'aka was taken by surprise and had his club only half-raised when Jason was upon him, and he swung wildly. Jason ducked under the blow and used Ch'aka's momentum to help throw him as he grabbed the club arm and pulled. Face down the armored man crashed against the stones and Jason was straddling his back even as he fell, clutching for his chin. He lacerated his fingers on a jagged tooth necklace then grasped the man's thick beard and pulled back. For a single long instant, before he could writhe free and roll over, Ch'aka's head was stretched back, and in that instant Jason plunged the sharp horn deep into the soft flesh of the throat. Hot blood burst over his hand and Ch'aka shuddered horribly under him and died.

Jason climbed wearily to his feet, suddenly exhausted. He was alone with his victim. The cold wind swept about them carrying the rustling grains of sand, chilling the sweat on his body. Sighing once he wiped his bloody hands on the sand and began to strip the corpse. Thick straps held the shell helmet over the dead man's head and when he unknotted them and pulled it away he saw that Ch'aka was well past middle age. There was some gray in his beard, but his scraggly hair was completely gray, his face and balding head pallid white from being concealed under the helmet. It took a long time to get the wrappings and armor off and retie them over himself, but it was finally done. Under the skin and claw wrappings on Ch'aka's feet were Jason's boots, filthy but undamaged, and Jason drew them on happily. When at last, after scouring it out with sand, he had strapped on the helmet, Ch'aka was reborn. The corpse on the sand was just another dead slave. Jason scraped a shallow grave, interred and covered it. Then, slung about with weapons, bags and crossbow, the club in his hand, he stalked back to the waiting slaves. As soon as he appeared they scrambled to their feet and formed a line. Jason saw Ijale looking at him worriedly, trying to discover who had won the battle.

"Score one for the visiting team," he called out, and she gave him a small, frightened smile and turned away. "About face all and head back the way we came. There is a new day dawning for you slaves. I know you don't believe this yet, but there are some big changes in store."

He whistled while he strolled after the line and chewed happily on the first *krenoj* that was found.

VI

That evening they built a fire on the beach and Jason sat with his back to the safety of the sea. He took his helmet off, the thing was giving him a headache, and called Ijale over to him.

"I hear Ch'aka. I obey."

She ran hurriedly over to him and flopped onto the sand.

"I want to talk to you," Jason said. "And my name is Jason, not Ch'aka."

"Yes, Ch'aka," she said, darting a quick glance at his exposed face, then turning away. He grumbled and pushed the basket of *krenoj* over to her.

"I can see where it is not going to be an easy thing changing this social setup. Tell me, do you or any of the others ever have any desire to be free?"

"What is free?"

"Well ... I suppose that answers my question. Free is what you are when you are not a slave, or a slave owner, free to go where you want and do what you want."

50

"I wouldn't like that." She shivered. "Who would take care of me? How could I find any *krenoj*? It takes many people together to find *krenoj*, one alone would starve."

"If you are free, you can combine with other free people and look for *krenoj* together."

"That is stupid. Whoever found would eat and not share unless a master made him. I like to eat."

Jason rasped his sprouting beard. "We all like to eat, but that doesn't mean we have to be slaves. But I can see that unless there are some radical changes in this environment I am not going to have much luck in freeing anyone, and I had better take all the precautions of a Ch'aka to see that I can stay alive."

He picked up his club and stalked off into the darkness, silently circling the camp until he found a good-sized knoll with smooth sides. Working by touch he pulled the little pegs from their bag and planted them in rows, carefully laying the leather strings in their forked tops. The ends of the strings were fastened to delicately balanced steel bells that tinkled at the slightest touch. Thus protected he lay down in the center of his warning spiderweb and spent a restless night, half awake, waiting tensely for the bells to ring.

***

In the morning the march continued and they came to the barrier cairn, and when the slaves stopped Jason urged them past it. They did this happily, looking forward to witnessing a good fight for possession of the violated territory. Their hopes were justified when later in the day the other row of slaves was seen far off to the right, and a figure detached itself and ran towards them.

"Hate you, Ch'aka!" Fasimba shouted as he ran up, only this time he meant what he said. "Coming on my ground, I kill you!"

"Not yet," Jason called out. "And hate you, Fasimba, sorry I forgot the formalities. I don't want any of your land and the old treaty or whatever it is still holds. I just want to talk to you."

Fasimba stopped, but kept his stone hammer ready, very suspicious. "You got new voice, Ch'aka."

"I got new Ch'aka, old Ch'aka now pushing up the daisies. I want to trade back a slave from you and then we'll go."

"Ch'aka fight hard. You must be good fighter Ch'aka." He shook his hammer angrily. "Not as good as me, Ch'aka!"

"You're the tops, Fasimba, nine slaves out of ten want you for a master. Look, can't we get to the point, then I'll get my mob out of here." He looked at the row of approaching slaves, trying to pick out Mikah. "I want back the slave who had the hole in his head. I'll give you two slaves in trade, your choice. What do you say to that?"

"Good trade, Ch'aka. You pick one of mine, take the best, I'll take two of yours. But hole-in-head gone. Too much trouble. Talk all the time. I got sore foot from kicking him. Got rid of him."

"Did you kill him?"

"Don't waste slave. Traded him to the D'zertanoj. Got arrows. You want arrows?"

"Not this time, Fasimba, but thanks for the information." He rooted around in a pouch and pulled out a *krenoj*. "Here, have something to eat."

"Where you get poisoned *krenoj*?" Fasimba asked with interest. "I could use a poisoned *krenoj*."

"This isn't poisoned, it's perfectly edible, or at least as edible as these things ever are."

Fasimba laughed. "You pretty funny, Ch'aka. I give you one arrow for poisoned *krenoj*."

"You're on," Jason said throwing the *krenoj* to the ground between them. "But I tell you it is perfectly good."

"That's what I tell man I give it to. I got good use for a poisoned *krenoj*." He threw an arrow into the sand away from them and grabbed up the vegetable as he left.

When Jason picked up the arrow it bent, and he saw that it was rusted almost completely in two and that the break had been craftily covered by clay. "That's all right," he called after the retreating slaver, "just wait until your friend eats the *krenoj*."

***

The march continued, first back to the boundary cairn with the suspicious Fasimba dogging their steps. Only after Jason and his band had passed the border did the others return to their normal foraging. Then began the long walk to the borders of the inland desert. Since they had to search for *krenoj* as they went it took them the better part of three days to reach their destination. Jason merely started the line in the correct direction, but as soon as he was out of sight of the sea he had only a rough idea of the correct course, however he did not confide his ignorance to the slaves and they marched steadily on, along what was obviously a well-known route to them. Along the way they collected and consumed a good number of *krenoj*, found two wells from which they refilled the skin bags, and pointed out a huddled animal sitting by a hole that Jason, to their un-voiced disgust, managed to miss completely with a bolt from the crossbow.

On the morning of the third day Jason saw a line of demarcation on the flattened horizon and before the midday meal they came to a sea of billowing, bluish-gray sand. The ending of what he had been accustomed to thinking of as the desert was startling. Beneath their feet were yellow sand and gravel, while occasional shrubs managed a sickly existence as did some grass and the life-giving *krenoj*. Animals as well as men lived here and, ruthless though survival was, they were at least alive. In the wastes ahead no life was possible or visible, though there seemed to be no doubt that the D'zertanoj lived there. This must mean that though it looked unlimited—as Ijale believed it to be—there were probably arable lands on the other side. Mountains as well, if they weren't just clouds, since a line of gray peaks could just be made out on the distant horizon.

Edipon

"Where do we find the D'zertanoj?" he asked the nearest slave who merely scowled and looked away. Jason was having a problem with discipline. The slaves would not do a thing he asked unless he kicked them. Their conditioning had been so thorough that an order unaccompanied by a kick just wasn't an order and his continued reluctance to impose the physical coercion with the spoken command was just being taken as a sign of weakness. Already some of the burlier slaves were licking their lips and sizing him up. His efforts to improve the life of the slaves were being blocked completely by the slaves themselves. With a mumbled curse at the continued obduracy of the human race Jason sank the toe of his boot into the man.

"Find them there by big rock," was the immediate response.

There was a dark spot at the desert's edge in the indicated direction and when they approached Jason saw that it was an outcropping of rock that had been built up with a wall of bricks or boulders to a uniform height. A good number of men could be concealed behind that wall and he was not going to risk his precious slaves or even more precious skin anywhere near it. At his shout the line halted and settled to the sand while he stalked a few meters in front, settling his club in his hand and suspiciously examined the structure.

That there were unseen watchers was proven when a man appeared from around the corner and walked slowly towards Jason. He was dressed in loose-fitting robes and carried a basket on one arm, and when he had reached a point roughly halfway between Jason and the rock he had just quitted he halted and sat crosslegged in the sand, the basket at his side. Jason looked carefully in all directions and decided the position was safe enough. There were no places of concealment where armed men might have hidden and he had no fear of the single man. Club ready he walked out and stopped a full three paces from the other.

"Welcome, Ch'aka," the man said. "I was afraid we wouldn't be seeing you again after that little ... difficulty we had."

He remained seated while he talked, stroking the few strands of his scraggly beard. His head was shaven smooth and as sunburned and leathery brown as the rest of his face, the most prominent feature of which was the magnificent prow of a nose that terminated in flaring nostrils and was used as sturdy support for a pair of handmade sunglasses. They appeared to be carved completely of bone and fit tightly to the face, their flat, solid fronts were cut with thin transverse slashes. This eye protection, the things could only have been for weak eyes, and the network of wrinkles indicated the man was quite old and would present no danger to Jason.

"I want something," Jason said, in straightforward, Ch'akaish manner.

"A new voice and a new Ch'aka—I bid you welcome. The old one was a dog and I hope he died in great pain when you killed him. Now sit friend Ch'aka and drink with me." He carefully opened the basket and removed a stone crock and two crockery mugs.

"Where you get poison drink?" Jason asked, remembering his local manners. This *D'zertano* was a smart one and had been able to tell instantly from Jason's voice that there had been a change in slaves. "And what your name?"

"Edipon," the ancient said as, uninsulted, he put the drinking apparatus back into the basket. "What is it that you want—within reason that is? We always need slaves and we are always willing to trade."

"I want slave you got. I trade you two for one."

The seated man smiled coldly from behind the shelter of his nose. "It is not necessary to talk as ungrammatically as the coastal barbarians, since I can tell by your accent that you are a man of education. What slave is it that you want?"

"The one that you just received from Fasimba. He belongs to me." Jason abandoned his linguistic ruse and put himself even more on guard, taking a quick look around at the empty sands. This dried up old bird was a lot brighter than he looked and he would have to stay on guard.

"Is that all you want?" Edipon asked.

"All I can think of at this moment. You produce this slave and perhaps we can talk more business."

"I have an even better idea than that."

Edipon's laugh had very dirty overtones and Jason sprang back when the oldster put two fingers into his mouth and whistled shrilly between them. There was the rustle of shifting sand and Jason wheeled to see men apparently climbing out of the empty desert, pushing back wooden covers over which the sand had been smoothed. There were six of them, with shields and clubs, and Jason cursed his stupidity at meeting Edipon on a spot of the other's choosing. He swung his club behind him but the oldster was already scampering for the safety of the rock. Jason howled in anger and ran at the nearest man who was still only halfway out of his hiding place. The man took Jason's blow on his upraised shield and was toppled back into the pit by the force of it. Jason ran on but another was ahead of him, swinging his own war club in readiness. There was no way around so Jason ran into him at full speed with all of his pendant teeth and horns gnashing and clattering. The man fell back under the attack and Jason split his shield with his club, and would have done further damage except that the other men arrived at that moment and he had to face them.

It was a brief and wicked battle, with Jason giving just a little more than he received. Two of the attackers were down and a third holding his cracked head when the weight of numbers carried Jason to the ground. He called to his slaves for aid, then cursed them when they only remained seated, while his arms were pinioned with rope and his weapons stripped from his body. One of the victors waved to the slaves who now stood and docilely marched into the desert. Jason was dragged, snarling with rage, in the same direction.

***

There was a wide opening in the desert-facing side of the wall and once through it Jason's anger instantly vanished. Here was one of the *caroj* that Ijale had told him about: there could be no doubt of it. He could now understand how, to her uneducated eye, there could exist an uncertainty as to whether the thing was an animal or not. The vehicle was a good ten meters long, shaped roughly like a boat, and bore on the front a large and obviously false animal head covered with fur and resplendent with rows of carved teeth and glistening crystal eyes. There were hide coverings and not-too realistic legs hanging about the thing, surely not enough camouflage to fool a sophisticated six-year old.

This sort of disguise might be good enough to take in the ignorant savages, but the same civilized child would recognize this as a vehicle as soon as he saw the six large wheels below. They were cut with deep treads and made from some resilient looking substance. No motive power was visible, but Jason almost hooted with joy at the prominent stink of burnt fuel. This crude looking contrivance had some artificial source of power, which might be the product of a local industrial revolution or have been purchased from off-world traders. Either possibility offered the chance of eventual escape from this nameless planet.

The slaves, some of them cringing with terror of the unknown, were kicked up the gangplank and into the *caroj*. Four of the huskies who had subdued and bound Jason carried him up and dumped him onto the deck where he lay quietly and examined what could be seen of the desert-vehicle's mechanism. A post projected from the front of the deck and one of the men fitted what could only have been a tiller handle over the squared top of it. If this monolithic apparatus steered with the front pair of wheels it must be driven with the rear, so Jason flopped around on the deck until he could look towards the stern. A cabin, the width of the deck, was situated here, windowless and with a single inset door fitted with a grand selection of locks and bolts. Any doubt that this was the engine room was displaced by the black metal smokestack that rose up through the cabin roof.

"We are leaving," Edipon screeched and waved his thin arms in the air. "Bring in the entranceway. Narsisi stand forward to indicate the way to the *caroj*. Now—all pray as I go into the shrine to induce the sacred powers to move us towards Putl'ko." He started towards the cabin, then stopped to point to one of the club bearers. "Erebo you lazy sod, did you remember to fill the watercup of the gods this time, because they grow thirsty?"

"I filled it, I filled it," Erebo muttered, chewing on a looted *krenoj*.

***

Preparations made, Edipon went into the recessed doorway and pulled a concealing curtain over it. There was much clanking and rattling as the locks and bolts were opened and he let himself inside. Within a few minutes a black cloud of greasy smoke rolled out of the smokestack and was whipped away by the wind. Almost an hour passed before the sacred powers were ready to move, and they announced their willingness to proceed by screaming and blowing their white breath up in the air. Four of the slaves screamed counterpoint and fainted, while the rest looked as if they would be happier off dead. Jason had had some experience with primitive machines before so the safety valve on the boiler came as no great surprise. He was also prepared when the vehicle shuddered and began to move slowly out into the desert. From the amount of smoke and the quantity of steam escaping from under the stern he didn't think the engine was very efficient, but primitive as it was it moved the *caroj* and its load of passengers across the sand at a creeping yet steady pace.

There were more screams from the slaves, and a few tried to leap over the side but were clubbed down. The robe-wrapped D'zertanoj were firmly working their way through the ranks of the captives, pouring ladlefuls of dark liquid down their throats. The first ones to receive it were already slumped unconscious or dead, though the chances were better that they were unconscious since there was no reason for their captors to kill them after going to such lengths to get them in the first place. Jason believed this, but the terrified slaves did not have the solace of his philosophy so struggled on, thinking that they were fighting for their lives. When Jason's turn came he did not submit meekly, in spite of his beliefs, and managed to bite some fingers and kick one man in the stomach before they sat on him, held his nose and poured a measure of the burning liquid down his throat. It hurt and he was dizzy, and he tried to will himself to throw up, but this was the last thing that he remembered.

VII

"Drink some more of this," the voice said, and cold water splashed on Jason's face and some of it trickled down his throat making him cough. Something hard was pressing into his back and his wrists hurt. Memory seeped back slowly, the fight, the capture and the potion that had been forced upon him. When he opened his eyes he saw a flickering yellow lamp overhead, hung from a chain. He blinked at it and tried to gather enough energy to sit up. A familiar face swam in front of the light and Jason squinted his eyes at it and groaned.

"Is that you Mikah—or are you just part of a nightmare?"

"There is no escape from justice, Jason. It is I, and I have some grave questions to put to you."

Jason groaned again. "You're real all right. Even in a nightmare I wouldn't dare dream up any lines like that. But before the questions, how about telling me a thing or two about the local setup, you should know something since you have been a slave of the D'zertanoj longer than I have." Jason realized that the pain in his wrists came from heavy iron shackles. A chain passed through them and was stapled to a thick wooden bar on which his head had been resting. "Why the chains—and what is the local hospitality like?"

Mikah resisted the invitation to impart any vital information and returned irresistibly to his own topic.

"When I saw you last you were a slave of Ch'aka, and tonight you were brought in with the other slaves of Ch'aka and chained to the bar while you were unconscious. There was an empty place next to mine and I told them I would tend you if they placed you there, and they did. Now there is something I must know. Before they stripped you I saw that you were wearing the armor and helmet of Ch'aka. Where is the man—what happened to him?"

"Me Ch'aka," Jason rasped, and burst out coughing from the dryness in his throat. He took a long drink of water from the bowl. "You sound very vindictive, Mikah you old fraud. Where is all the turn-the-other-cheek stuff now? Don't tell me you could possibly hate the man just because he hit you on the head, fractured your skull and sold you down the river as a slave reject? In case you have been brooding over this injustice you can now be cheered because the evil Ch'aka is no more. He is buried in the trackless wastes and after all the applicants were sifted out I got the job."

"You killed him?"

"In a word—yes. And don't think that it was easy since he had all the advantages and I possessed only my native ingenuity, which luckily proved to be enough. It was touch and go for a while because when I tried to assassinate him in his sleep—"

"You *what*?" Mikah Samon hissed.

"Got to him at night. You don't think anyone in his right mind would tackle a monster like that face-to-face do you? Though it ended up that way, since he had some neat gadgets for keeping track of people in the dark. Briefly, we fought, I won, I became Ch'aka, though my reign was neither long nor noble. I followed you as far as the desert where I was neatly trapped by a shrewd old bird name of Edipon who demoted me back to the ranks and took away all my slaves as well. Now that's my story. So tell me yours, where we are, what goes on here?"

"Assassin! Slave holder!" Mikah reared back, as far as he could under the restraint of the chain, and pointed the finger of judgment at Jason. "Two more charges must be added to your role of infamy. I sicken myself, Jason, that I could ever have felt sympathy for you and tried to help you. I will still help you, but only to stay alive so that you may be taken back to Cassylia for trial and execution."

"I like that example of fair and impartial justice— trial *and* execution." Jason coughed again and drained the bowl of water. "Didn't you ever hear of presumed innocence until proven guilty? It only happens to be the mainstay of all jurisprudence. And how could you possibly justify trying me on Cassylia for actions that occurred on this planet—that aren't crimes here? That's like taking a cannibal away from his tribe and executing him for anthropophagy."

"What would be wrong with that? The eating of human flesh is a crime so loathsome I shudder to think of it. Of course a man who does that must be executed."

"If he slips in the back door and eats one of your relatives, you certainly have grounds for action. But not if he joins the rest of his jolly tribe for a good roast of enemy. Don't you see the obvious point here—that human conduct can only be judged in relation to its environment? Conduct is relative. The cannibal in his society is just as moral as the churchgoer in yours."

"Blasphemer! A crime is a crime! There are moral laws that stand above all human society."

"Oh no there are not, that's just the point where your medieval morality breaks down. All laws and ideas are historical and relative, not absolute. They are relevant to their particular time and place and taken out of context they lose their importance. Within the context of this grubby society I acted in a most straightforward and honest manner. I attempted to assassinate my master—which is the only way an ambitious boy can get ahead in this hard world, and which was undoubtedly the way Ch'aka himself got the job in the first place. Assassination didn't work but combat did, and the results were the same. Once in power I took good care of my slaves, though of course they didn't appreciate it since they didn't want good care, they only wanted my job, that being the law of the land. The only thing I really did wrong was to not live up to my obligations as a slave holder and keep them marching up and down the beaches forever. Instead I came looking for you and was trapped and broken back to slavery where I belong for pulling such a stupid trick."

The door crashed open and harsh sunlight streamed into the windowless building. "On your feet slaves!" a D'zertano shouted in through the opening.

A chorus of shufflings and groans broke out as the men stirred to life. Jason could see now that he was one of twenty slaves shackled to the long bar, apparently the entire trunk of a good-sized tree. The man chained at the far end seemed to be a leader of sorts because he cursed and goaded the others to life. When they were all standing he snapped his commands in a hectoring tone of voice.

"Come on, come on, first come best food. And don't forget your bowls, put them away so they can't drop out, remember nothing to eat or drink all day unless you have a bowl. And let's work together today, everyone pull his weight, that's the only way to do it. That goes for all you men, specially you new men. Give them a day's work here and they give you a day's food...."

"Oh shut up!" someone shouted.

"... And you can't complain about that," the strawboss whined on, unperturbed. "Now altogether ... *one* ... bend down and get your hands around the bar, get a good grip and ... *two* ... lift it clear of the ground, that's the way. And ... *three* ... stand up and out the door we go."

They shuffled out into the sunlight and the cold wind of dawn bit through his Pyrran coverall and the remnants of Ch'aka's leather trappings that Jason had been allowed to keep. His captors had torn off the claw-studded feet but not bothered the wrappings underneath, so they hadn't found his boots. This was the only bright spot on an otherwise unlimited vista of blackest gloom. Jason tried to be thankful for small blessings, but only shivered some more. As soon as possible this situation had to be changed since he had already served his term as slave on this backwoods planet and was cut out for better things.

On order the slaves lined up against the walls of the yard. Presenting their bowls like scruffy penitents they accepted dippers of lukewarm soup from another slave who pushed along a wheeled tub of the stuff: he was chained to the tub. Jason's appetite vanished when he tasted the sludge. It was *krenoj* soup, and the desert tubers tasted even worse—he hadn't thought it was possible—when served up in a broth. But survival was more important than fastidiousness, so he gulped the evil stuff down.

***

Breakfast over they marched out the gate into another compound and fascinated interest displaced all of Jason's concerns. In the center of the yard was a large capstan into which the first group of slaves were already fitting the end of their bar. Jason's group, and the two others, shuffled into position and seated their bars, making a four spoked wheel out of the capstan. An overseer shouted and the slaves groaned and threw their weight against the bars until they shuddered and began to turn, then trudging slowly they kept the wheel moving. Once this slogging labor was under way Jason turned his attention to the crude mechanism that they were powering.

A vertical shaft from the capstan turned a creaking wooden wheel that set a series of leather belts into motion. Some of them vanished through openings into a large stone building, while the strongest strap of all turned the rocker arm of what could only be a counterbalanced pump. This all seemed like a highly inefficient way to go about pumping water since there certainly must be natural springs and lakes somewhere around. The pungent smell that filled the yard was hauntingly familiar, and Jason had just reached the conclusion that water couldn't be the object of their labors when a throaty gurgling came from the standpipe of the pump and a thick black stream bubbled out.

"Petroleum—of course!" Jason enthused out loud, then bent his attentions to pushing when the overseer gave him an ugly look and cracked his whip menacingly.

This was the secret of the D'zertanoj, and the source of their power. Mountains were visible nearby, and hills, towering above the surrounding walls. The captured slaves had been drugged so they would not even know in which direction they had been brought to this hidden site, or how long the trip was. Here in this guarded valley they labored to pump the crude oil that their masters used to power their big desert wagons. Or did they use crude oil for this?

64

The petroleum was gurgling out in a solid stream now, and running down an open trough that vanished through the wall into the same building as the turning belts. And what barbaric devilishness went on in there? A thick chimney crowned the building and produced clouds of black smoke, while from the various openings in the wall came a tremendous stench that threatened to lift the top off his head.

At the same moment that he realized what was going on in the building a guarded door was opened and Edipon came out, blowing his sizable nose in a scrap of rag. The creaking wheel turned and when its rotation brought Jason around again he called out to him.

"Hey, Edipon, come over here. I want to talk to you. I'm the former Ch'aka, in case you don't recognize me out of uniform."

Edipon gave him one look, then turned away dabbing at his nose. It was obvious that slaves held no interest for him, no matter what their position had been before their fall. The slave-driver ran over with a roar, raising his whip, while the slow rotation of the wheel carried Jason away. He shouted back over his shoulder.

"Listen to me—I know a lot and can help you." Only a turned back for an answer and the whip was already whistling down. It was time for the hard sell. "You had better hear me—because I know that *what comes out first is best*. Yeow!" This last was involuntary as the whip landed.

Jason's words were without meaning to the slaves as well as the overseer who was raising his whip for another blow, but their impact on Edipon was as dramatic as if he had stepped on a hot coal. He shuddered to a halt and wheeled about, and even at this distance Jason could see that a sickly gray tone had replaced his normal browned color of his skin.

"*Stop the wheel!*" he shouted.

***

This unexpected command drew the startled attention of everyone.

The gape-mouthed overseer lowered his whip while the slaves stumbled and halted and the wheel groaned to a stop. In the sudden silence Edipon's steps echoed loudly as he ran to Jason, halting a hand's breadth away, his lips drawn back from his teeth with tension as if he were prepared to bite.

"What was that you said?" He hurled the words at Jason while his fingers half-plucked a knife from his belt.

Jason smiled, looking and acting calmer than he felt. His barb had gone home, but unless he proceeded carefully so would Edipon's knife—into his stomach. This was obviously a very sensitive topic.

"You heard what I said—and I don't think you want me to repeat it in front of all these strangers. I know what happens here because I come from a place far away where we do this kind of thing all the time. I can help you. I can show you how to get more of the best, and how to make your *caroj* work better. Just try me. Only unchain me from this bar first and let's get to some place private where we can have a nice chat."

Edipon's thoughts were obvious. He chewed his lip and looked hotly at Jason, fingering the edge of his knife. Jason only returned a smile of pure innocence and tapped his fingers happily on the bar, just marking time while he waited to be released. Yet in spite of the cold there was a rivulet of sweat trickling down his spine. He was gambling everything on Edipon's intelligence, that the man's curiosity would overcome the immediate desire to silence the slave who knew so much about things so secret, hoping that he would remember that slaves could always be killed, and that it wouldn't hurt to ask a few questions first. Curiosity won and the knife dropped back into the sheath while Jason let his breath out in a relieved sigh. It had been entirely too close, even for a professional gambler; his own life on the board was a little higher stakes than he enjoyed playing for.

"Release him from the bar and bring him to me," Edipon ordered, then strode agitatedly away. The other slaves watched wide-eyed as the blacksmith was rushed out, and with much confusion and shouted orders Jason's chain was cut from the bar where it joined the heavy staple.

"What are you doing?" Mikah asked, and one of the guards backhanded him to the ground. Jason just smiled and touched his finger to his lips as his chain was released and they led him away. He was free from bondage and he would stay that way if he could convince Edipon that he would be better off in some capacity other than dumb labor.

***

The room they led him to contained the first touches of decoration or self-indulgence that he had seen on this planet. The furniture was carefully constructed, with an occasional bit of carving to brighten it, and there was a woven cover on the bed. Edipon stood by a table, tapping his fingers nervously on the dark polished surface. "Lock him up," he ordered the guards, and Jason was secured to a sturdy ringbolt that projected from the wall. As soon as the guards were gone he stood before Jason and drew his knife. "Tell me what you know or I will kill you at once."

"My past is an open book to you, Edipon. I come from a land where we know all the secrets of nature—"

"What is the name of this land? Are you a spy from Appsala?"

"I couldn't very well be one since I have never heard of the place." Jason pulled at his lower lip, wondering just how intelligent Edipon was, and just how frank he could be with him. This was no time to get tangled up in lies about planetary geography: it might be best to try him on a small dose of the truth. "If I told you I came from another planet, another world in the sky up among the stars, would you believe me?"

"Perhaps. There are many old legends that our forefathers came from a world beyond the sky, but I have always dismissed this as religious drivel, fit only for women."

"In this case the girls happen to be right. Your planet was settled by

67

men whose ships crossed the emptiness of space as your *caroj* pass over the desert. Your people have forgotten about that and lost the science and knowledge you once had, but in other worlds the knowledge is still held."

"Madness!"

"Not at all, it is science, though many times confused as being the same thing. I'll prove my point. You know that I could never have been inside your mysterious building out there, and I imagine you can be sure no one has told me its secrets. Yet I'll bet you that I can describe fairly accurately what is in there—not from seeing the machinery, but from knowing what must be done to oil in order to get the products you need. Do you want to hear?"

"Proceed," Edipon said, sitting on a corner of the table and balancing the knife loosely in his palm.

"I don't know what you call it, the device, but in the trade it is a pot still used for fractional distillation. Your crude oil runs into a tank of some kind, and you pipe it from there to a retort, some big vessel that you can seal airtight. Once it is closed you light a fire under the thing and try to get all the oil to an even temperature. A gas rises from the oil and you take it off through a pipe and run it through a condenser, probably more pipe with water running over it. Then you put a bucket under the open end of the pipe and out of it drips the juice that you burn in your *caroj* to make them move."

Edipon's eyes opened wider and wider while Jason talked until they stuck out of his head like boiled eggs. "Demon!" he screeched and tottered towards Jason with the knife extended. "You couldn't have seen, not through stone walls, yet only my family have seen, no others—I'll swear to that!"

"Keep cool, Edipon, I told you that we have been doing this stuff for years in my country." He balanced on one foot, ready for a kick at the knife in case the old man's nerves did not settle down. "I'm not out to steal your secrets, in fact they are pretty small potatoes where I come from since every farmer has a still for cooking up his own mash and saving on taxes. I'll bet I can even put in some improvements for you, sight unseen. How do you monitor the temperature on your cooking brew? Do you have thermometers?"

"What are thermometers?" Edipon asked, forgetting the knife for the moment, drawn on by the joys of a technical discussion.

"That's what I thought. I can see where your bootleg joyjuice is going to take a big jump in quality, if you have anyone here who can do some simple glassblowing. Though it might be easier to rig up a coiled bi-metallic strip. You're trying to boil off your various fractions, and unless you keep an even and controlled temperature you are going to have a mixed brew. The thing you want for your engines are the most volatile fractions, the liquids that boil off first like gasoline and benzene. After that you raise the temperature and collect kerosene for your lamps and so forth right on down the line until you have a nice mass of tar left to pave your roads with. How does that sound to you?"

***

Edipon had forced himself into calmness, though a jumping muscle in his cheek betrayed his inner tension. "What you have described is the truth, though you were wrong on some small things. But I am not interested in your thermometer nor in improving our water-of-power, it has been good enough for my family for generations and it is good enough for me...."

"I bet you think that line is original?"

"... There is something that you might be able to do that would bring you rich rewards. We can be generous when needs be. You have seen our *caroj* and ridden on one, and seen me go into the shrine to intercede with the sacred powers to make us move. Can you tell me what power moves the *caroj*?"

"I hope this is the final exam, Edipon, because you are stretching my powers of extrapolation. Stripping away all the *shrines* and *sacred powers* I would say that you go into the engine room to do a piece of work with very little praying involved. There could be a number of

69

ways of moving those barns, but let's think of the simplest. This is top of the head now, so no penalties if I miss any of the fine points.

"Internal combustion is out, I doubt if you have the technology to handle it, plus the fact there was a lot to do about the water tank and it took you almost an hour to get under way. That sounds like you were getting up a head of steam—the safety valve! I forgot about that. So it is steam. You go in, lock the door of course, then open a couple of valves until the fuel drips into the firebox, then you light it. Maybe you have a pressure gauge, or maybe you just wait until the safety valve pops to tell you if you have a head of steam. Which can be dangerous since a sticking valve could blow the whole works right over the mountain.

"Once you have the steam you crack a valve to let it into the cylinders and get the thing moving. After that you just enjoy the trip, of course making sure the water is feeding to your boiler all right, that your pressure stays up, your fire is hot enough, all your bearings are lubricated and the rest...."

Jason looked on astounded as Edipon did a little jig around the room, holding his robe up above his bony knees. Bouncing with excitement he jabbed his knife into the table top and rushed over to Jason and grabbed him by the shoulders, shaking him until his chain rattled.

"Do you know what you have done?" he asked. "Do you know what you have said?"

"I know well enough. Does this mean that I have passed the exam? Was I right?"

"I don't know if you are right or not. I have never seen the inside of one of the Appsalan devil-boxes." He danced around the room again. "You know more about their ... what do you call it, *engine* ... than I do. I have only spent my life tending them and cursing the people of Appsala who keep the secret from us. But you will reveal it to us! We will build our own engines and if they want water-of-power they will have to pay dearly for it."

"Would you mind being a little bit clearer," Jason pleaded. "I have never heard anything so confused in my entire life."

"I will show you, man from a far world, and you will reveal the Appsalan secrets to us. I see the dawn of a new day for Putl'ko arriving." He opened the door and shouted for the guards, and for his son, Narsisi, who arrived as they were unlocking Jason who recognized him as the same droop-eyed and sleepy looking D'zertano who had been helping Edipon to drive their ungainly vehicle.

"Seize this chain my son and keep your club ready to kill this slave if he makes any attempt to escape. Otherwise do not harm him, for he is very valuable. Come."

He tugged on the chain, but Jason only dug his heels in and did not move. They looked at him, astonished.

"Just a few things before we go. The man who is to bring the new day to Putl'ko is not a slave, let us get that straight before this operation goes any further. We'll work out something with chains or guards so I can't escape, but the slavery thing is out."

"But—you are not one of us, therefore you must be a slave."

"I've just added a third category to your social order. Employee. Though reluctant, I am still an employee, skilled labor, and I intend to be treated that way. Figure it out for yourself. Kill a slave and what do you lose? Very little if there is another slave in the pens that can push in the same place. But kill me and what do you get? Brains on your club—and they do you no good at all there."

"Say, Dad, does he mean I can't kill him?" Narsisi looked puzzled as well as sleepy.

"No, he doesn't mean that. He means if we kill him there is no one else that can do the work he is to do for us. I can understand him and I do not like it. There are only slaves and slavers, anything else is against the natural order. But he has us trapped between *satano* and the sand-storm so we must allow him some freedoms. Bring the slave now ... I mean the employee ... and we will see if he can do the things he has promised. If he does not, *I* will have the pleasure of killing him because I do not like his revolutionary ideas."

***

They marched single file to a locked and guarded building with immense doors, which were pulled open to reveal the massive forms of seven *caroj*.

"Look at them," Edipon hissed and tugged at his nose. "The finest and most beautiful of constructions, striking fear into our enemies' hearts, carrying us fleetly across the sands, bearing on their backs immense loads and only three of the things are able to move."

"Engine trouble?" Jason asked lightly.

Edipon grumbled, cursed and fumed under his breath and led the way to an inner courtyard where stood four immense black boxes painted with death-heads, splintered bones, fountains of blood and cabalistic symbols all of a sinister appearance.

"Those swine in Appsala take our water-of-power and give nothing in return. Oh yes, they let us use their engines, but after running for a few months the cursed things stop and will not go again, then we must bring them back to the city to exchange for a new one, and pay again and again."

"A nice racket," Jason said, looking at the sealed covering on the engines. "Why don't you just crack into them and fix them yourself, they can't be very complex."

"That is death!" Edipon gasped, and both D'zertanoj recoiled from the boxes at the thought. "We have tried that, in my father's father's day, since we are not superstitious like the slaves and know that

72

these are man-made not god-made. However the tricky serpents of Appsala hide their secrets with immense cunning. If any attempt is made to break the covering horrible death leaks out and fills the air. Men who breathe the air die, and even those who are solely touched by it develop immense blisters and die in pain. The man of Appsala laughed when this happened to our people and after that raised the price even higher."

Jason circled one of the boxes, examining it with interest, trailing Narsisi behind him at the end of the chain. The thing was higher than his head and almost twice as long. A heavy shaft emerged through openings on opposite sides, probably the power takeoff for the wheels. Through an opening in the side he could see inset handles and two small colored disks, and above this were three funnel-shaped openings shaped and painted like mouths. By standing on tiptoe Jason looked on top but there was only a flanged, sooty opening that must be for attachment of a smokestack. There was only one more opening, a smallish one in the rear, and no other controls on the garish container.

"I'm beginning to get the picture, but you will have to tell me how you work the controls."

"Death before that," Narsisi shouted. "Only my family—"

"Will you shut up!" Jason shouted right back. "Remember? You're not allowed to browbeat the help anymore. There are no secrets here. Not only that, but I probably know more about this thing than you do just by looking at it. Oil, water and fuel go in these three openings, you poke a light in somewhere, probably in that smoky hole under the controls, open one of those valves for fuel supply, another one is to make the engine go slower and faster, and the third is for your water feed. The disks are indicators of some kind." Narsisi paled and stepped back. "So keep the trap shut while I talk to your dad."

"It is as you say," Edipon pointed. "The mouths must always be filled and woebetide if they shall go empty for the powers will halt or worse. Fire goes in here as you guessed, and when the green finger comes forward this lever may be turned for motion. The next is for great speed or going slow. The very last is under the sign of the red finger, which when it points indicates need, and the handle must be turned and held until the finger retires. White breath comes from the opening in back. That is all there is."

"About what I expected," Jason muttered and examined the container wall, rapping it with his knuckles until it boomed. "They give you the minimum of controls to run the thing, so you won't learn anything about the basic principles involved. Without the theory you would never know what the handles control, or that the green indicator comes out when you have operating pressure or the red one when the water level is low in the boiler. Very neat. And the whole thing sealed up in a can and booby-trapped in case you have any ideas of going into business for yourself.

"The cover sounds like it is double walled, and from your description I would say that it has one of the vesicant war gases, like mustard gas, sealed inside there in liquid form. Anyone who tries to cut their way in will quickly forget their ambitions after a dose of that. Yet there must be a way to get inside the case and service the engine, they aren't just going to throw them away after a few months' use. And considering the level of technology displayed by this monstrosity I should be able to find the tricks and get around any other built-in traps. I think I'll take the job."

"Very well, begin."

"Wait a minute, boss, you still have a few things to learn about hired labor. There are always certain working conditions and agreements involved, all of which I'll be happy to list for you."

VIII

"What I do not understand is why you must have the other slave?" Narsisi whined. "To have the woman of course is natural, as well as to have quarters of your own, my father has given his permission.

But he also said that I and my brothers are to help you, that the secrets of the engine are to be revealed to no one else."

"Then trot right over to him and get permission for the slave Mikah to join me in the work. You can explain that he comes from the same land that I do, and that your secrets are mere children's toys to him. And if dad wants any other reasons tell him that I need skilled aid, someone who knows how to handle tools and who can be trusted to follow directions exactly as given. You and your brothers have entirely too many ideas of your own about how things should be done, and a tendency to leave details up to the gods and have a good bash with the hammer if things don't work the way they should."

Narsisi retired, seething and mumbling to himself while Jason huddled over the oil stove planning the next step. It had taken most of the day to lay down logs for rollers and to push the sealed engine out into the sandy valley, far from the well site; open space was needed for any experiments where a mistake could release a cloud of war gas. Even Edipon had finally seen the sense of this, though all of his tendencies were to conduct the experiments with great secretiveness behind locked doors. He had granted permission only after skin walls had been erected to form an enclosure that could be guarded; it was only incidental that they acted as a much-appreciated windbreak.

And after much argument the dangling chains and shackles had been removed from Jason's arms and light-weight leg-irons substituted. He had to shuffle when he walked but his arms were completely free, a great improvement over the chains, even though one of the brothers kept watch with a cocked crossbow as long as Jason wasn't fastened down. Now he had to get some tools and some idea of the technical knowledge of these people before he could proceed, which would necessarily entail one more battle over their precious secrets.

"Come on," he called to his guard, "let's find Edipon and give his ulcers another twinge."

After his first enthusiasm the leader of the D'zertanoj was getting very little pleasure out of his new project.

"You have quarters of your own," he grumbled, "and the slave woman to cook for you, and I have just given permission for the other slave to help you. Now more requests—do you want to drain all the blood from my body?"

"Let's not dramatize too much. I simply want some tools to get on with my work, and a peek at your machine shop or wherever it is you do your mechanical work. I have to have some idea of the way you people solve mechanical problems before I can go to work on that box of tricks out there in the desert."

"Entrance is forbidden—"

"Regulations are snapping like straws today, so we might as well go on and finish off a few more. Will you lead the way?"

The guards were reluctant to open the refinery building gates to Jason, and there was much rattling of keys and worried looks. A brace of elderly D'zertanoj, stinking of oil fumes, emerged from the interior and joined in a shouted argument with Edipon whose will finally prevailed. Chained again, and guarded like a murderer, Jason was begrudgingly led into the dark interior, the contents of which was depressingly anticlimactic.

"Really from rubeville," Jason sneered and kicked at the boxful of hand-forged and clumsy tools. The work was of the crudest, the product of a sort of neolithic machine age. The distilling retort had been laboriously formed from sheet copper and clumsily riveted together. It leaked mightily as did the soldered seams on the hand-formed pipe. Most of the tools were blacksmith's tongs and hammers for heating and beating out shapes on the anvil. The only things that gladdened Jason's heart were the massive drill press and lathe that worked off the slave-power drive belts. In the tool holder of the lathe was clamped a chip of some hard mineral that did a good enough job of cutting the forged iron and low-carbon steel. Even more cheering was the screw-thread advance on the cutting head that was used to produce the massive nuts and bolts that secured the *caroj* wheels to their shafts. It could have been worse. Jason sorted out the smallest and handiest tools and put them aside for his own use in the morning. The light was almost gone and there would be no more work this day.

***

They left, in armed procession, as they came, and a brace of brothers showed him to the kennellike room that was to be his private quarters. The heavy bolt thudded shut in the door behind him and he winced at the thick fumes of half-burnt kerosene through which the light of the single-wick lamp barely penetrated. Ijale crouched over the small oil stove cooking something in a pottery bowl. She looked up and smiled hesitatingly at Jason, then turned back to the stove. Jason walked over, sniffed and shuddered.

"What a feast! *Krenoj* soup, and I suppose followed by fresh *krenoj* and *krenoj* salad. Tomorrow I see about getting a little variety into the diet."

"Ch'aka is great," she whispered without looking up. "Ch'aka is powerful...."

"Jason is the name, I lost the Ch'aka job when they took the uniform away."

"... Jason is powerful to work charms on the D'zertanoj and makes them do what he will. His slave thanks you."

He lifted her chin and the dumb obedience in her eyes made him wince. "Can't we forget about the slavery bit? We are in this thing together and we'll get out of it together."

"We will escape, I knew it. You will kill all the D'zertanoj and release your slaves and lead us home again where we can march and find *krenoj* far from this terrible place."

"Some girls are sure easy to please. That is roughly what I had in mind, except when we get out of here we are going in the other direction, as far away from your *krenoj* crowd as I can get."

77

Ijale listened attentively, stirring the soup with one hand and scratching inside her leather wrappings with the other. Jason found himself scratching as well, and realized from sore spots on his hide that he had been doing an awful lot of this since he had been dragged out of the ocean of this inhospitable planet.

"Enough is enough!" he exploded and went over and hammered on the door. "This place is a far cry from civilization as I know it, but that is no reason why we can't be as comfortable as possible." Chains and bolts rattled outside the door and Narsisi pushed his gloom-ridden face in.

"Why do you cry out? What is wrong?"

"I need some water, lots of it."

"But you have water," Narsisi said, puzzled, and pointed to a stone crock in the corner. "There is water there enough for days."

"By your standards, Nars old boy, not mine. I want at least ten times as much as that and I want it now. And some soap, if there is such stuff in this barbaric place."

There was a good deal of argument involved, but Jason finally got his way with the water by explaining it was needed for religious rites to make sure that he would not fail in the work tomorrow. It came in a varied collection of containers along with a shallow bowl full of powerful soft soap.

"We're in business," he chortled. "Take your clothes off, I have a surprise for you."

"Yes, Jason," Ijale said, smiling happily.

"You're going to get a bath. Do you know what a bath is?"

"No," she said, and shuddered. "It sounds evil."

"Over here and off with the clothes," he ordered, poking at a hole in the floor. "This should serve as a drain, at least the water went away when I poured some into it."

The water was warm from the stove, yet Ijale still crouched against the wall and shuddered when he poured it over her. She screamed when he rubbed the slippery soap into her hair, and he continued with his hand over her mouth so that she wouldn't bring in the guards. He rubbed the soap into his own head, too, and it tingled delightfully as it soaked through to his scalp. Some of it was in his ears, muffling them, so the first intimation he had that the door was opened was the sound of Mikah's hoarse shout. He was standing in the doorway, finger pointed and shaking with wrath. Narsisi was standing behind him, peering over his shoulder with fascination at this weird religious rite.

"Degradation!" Mikah thundered. "You force this poor creature to bend to your will, humiliate her, strip her clothes from her and gaze upon her though you are not united in lawful wedlock." He shielded his eyes from sight with a raised arm. "You are evil, Jason, a demon of evil and must be brought to justice—"

"*Out!*" Jason roared, and spun Mikah about and started him through the door with one of his practiced Ch'aka kicks. "The only evil here is in your mind, you snooping scut. I'm giving the girl the first scrubbing of her life and you should be giving me a medal for bringing sanitation to the natives instead of howling like that." He pushed them both out the door and shouted at Narsisi. "I wanted this slave, but not *now*! Lock him up until morning then bring him back." He slammed the door and made a mental note to get hold of a bolt to be placed on this side as well.

***

There were more *krenoj* for breakfast but Jason was feeling too good physically to mind. He was scrubbed raw and clean and the itching was gone even from his sprouting beard. The metalcloth of his Pyrran coverall had dried almost as soon as it had been washed so he was wearing clean clothes as well. Ijale was still recovering from the traumatic effects of her bath, but she looked positively attractive with her skin cleaned and her hair washed and combed a bit. He would have to find some of the local cloth for her since it would be a shame to ruin the good work by letting her get back into the badly cured skins she was used to wearing. It was with a sensation of positive good feeling that he bellowed for the door to be opened and stamped through the cool morning to his place of labor. Mikah was already there, looking scruffy and angry as he rattled his chains; Jason gave him the friendliest of smiles that only rubbed salt into the other's moral wounds.

"Leg-irons for him, too," Jason ordered, "And do it fast. We have a big job to do today." He turned back to the sealed engine, rubbing his hands together with anticipation.

The concealing hood was made of thin metal that could not hide many secrets. He carefully scratched away some of the paint and discovered a crimped and soldered joint where the sides met, but no other revealing marks. After an hour spent tapping all over with his ear pressed to the metal he was sure that the hood was just what he had thought it was when he first examined the thing—a double-walled metal container filled with liquid. Puncture it and you were dead. It was there merely to hide the secrets of the engine, and served no other function. Yet it had to be passed to service the steam engine—or did it? The construction was roughly cubical, and the hood covered only five sides. What about the sixth, the base?

"Now you're thinking, Jason," he chortled to himself, and knelt down to examine it. A wide flange, apparently of cast iron, projected all around, and was penetrated by four large bolt holes. The protective casing seemed to be soldered to the base, but there must be stronger concealed attachments because it would not move even after he carefully scratched away some of the solder at the base. Therefore the answer simply had to be on the sixth side.

"Over here, Mikah," he called, and the man detached himself reluctantly from the warmth of the stove and shuffled up. "Come close and look at this medieval motive-power while we talk, as if we are discussing business. Are you going to co-operate with me?"

"I do not want to, Jason. I am afraid that you will soil me with your touch, as you have others."

"Well you're not so clean now—"

"I do not mean physically."

"Well I do. You could certainly do with a bath and a deep shampoo. I'm not worried about the state of your soul, you can battle that out on your own time. But if you work with me I'll find a way to get us out of this place and to the city that made this engine, because if there is a way off this planet we'll find it only in the city."

"I know that, yet I still hesitate—"

"Small sacrifices now for the greater good later. Isn't the entire purpose of this trip to get me back to justice? You're not going to accomplish that by rotting out the rest of your life as a slave."

"You are the devil's advocate the way you twist my conscience—yet what you say is true. I will help you here so that we can escape."

"Fine. Now get to work. Take Narsisi and have him round up at least three good-sized poles, the kind we were chained to in the pumping gang. Bring them back here along with a couple of shovels."

***

Slaves carried the poles only as far as the outside of the skin walls, since Edipon would not admit them inside, and it was up to Jason and Mikah to drag them laboriously to the site. The D'zertanoj, who never did physical labor, thought it was very funny when Jason suggested that they help. Once in position by the engine, Jason dug channels beneath it and forced the bars under. When this was done he took turns with Mikah in digging out the sand beneath until the engine stood over a pit supported only by the bars. Jason let himself down and examined the bottom of the machine. It was smooth and featureless.

Once more he scratched away the paint with careful precision, until it was cleared around the edges. Here the solid metal gave way to solder and he picked at this until he discovered that a piece of sheet metal had been soldered at the edges and fastened to the bedplate.

"Very tricky, these Appsalanoj," he chortled and attacked the solder with a knife blade. When one end was loose he slowly pulled the sheet of metal away, making positive that there was nothing attached to it, nor that it had been booby-trapped in any way. It came off easily enough and clanged down into the pit. The revealed surface was smooth metal, featureless and hard.

"Enough for one day," Jason said, climbing out of the pit and brushing off his hands. It was almost dark. "We've accomplished enough for now and I want to think a bit before I go ahead. So far luck has been on our side, but I don't think it should be this easy. I hope you brought your suitcase with you, Mikah, because you're moving in with me."

"Never! A sink of sin, depravity—"

Jason looked him coldly in the eye and with each word he spoke he stabbed him in the chest with his finger to drive home the point. "You are moving in with me because that is essential to our plans. And if you stop referring to my moral weaknesses I'll stop talking about yours. Now come on."

Living with Mikah Samon was trying, but barely possible. He made Ijale and Jason go to the far wall and turn their backs and promise not to look while he bathed behind a screen of skins. Jason did this but exacted a small revenge by telling Ijale jokes so that they tittered together and Mikah would be sure they were laughing at him. The screen of skins remained after the bath, and was reinforced, and Mikah retired behind it to sleep. Their food still consisted only of *krenoj* and Jason shuddered while he admitted that he was actually growing used to them.

The following morning, under the frightened gaze of his guards, Jason tackled the underside of the baseplate. He had been thinking about it a good part of the night and he put his theories to the test at once. By pressing hard on a knife he could make a good groove in the metal. It was not as soft as the solder, but seemed to be some simple alloy containing a good percentage of lead. What could it be concealing? Probing carefully with the point of the knife he covered the bottom in a regular pattern. The depth of the metal was uniformly deep except in two spots where he found irregularities, they were on the midline of the rectangular base, and equidistant from the ends and sides. Picking and scraping he uncovered two familiar looking shapes each as big as his head.

"Mikah. Get down in this hole and look at these things. Tell me what you think they are."

Mikah scratched his beard. "They're still covered with this metal, I can't be sure—"

"I'm not asking you to be sure of anything—just tell me what they make you think of."

"Why ... big nuts of course. Threaded on the ends of bolts. But they are so big—"

"They would have to be if they hold the entire metal case on. I think we are getting very close now to the mystery of how to open the engine—and this is the time to be careful. I still can't believe it is as easy as this to crack the secret. I'm going to whittle a wooden template of the nut, then have a wrench made. While I'm gone you stay down here and pick all the metal off the bolt and out of the screw threads. I can put off doing it while we think this thing through, but sooner or later I'm going to have to take a stab at turning one of those nuts. And I find it very hard to forget about that mustard gas."

Making the wrench put a small strain on the local technology and all of the old men who enjoyed the title of Masters of the Still went into consultation over it. One of them was a fair blacksmith and after a ritual sacrifice and a round of prayers he shoved a bar of iron into the charcoal and Jason pumped the bellows until it glowed white hot. With much hammering and cursing it was laboriously formed into a sturdy open-end wrench with an offset head to get at the countersunk nuts. Jason made sure that the opening was slightly undersized, then took the untempered wrench to the work site and filed the jaws to an exact fit. After being reheated and quenched in oil he had the tool that he hoped would do the job.

***

Edipon must have been keeping track of the work progress because he was waiting near the engine when Jason returned with the completed wrench.

"I have been under," he announced, "and have seen the nuts that the devilish Appsalanoj have concealed within solid metal. Who would have suspected! It still seems to me impossible that one metal could be hidden within another, how could that be done?"

"Easy enough. The base of the assembled engine was put into a form and the molten covering metal poured into it. It must have a much lower melting point than the steel of the engine so there would be no damage. They just have a better knowledge of metal technology in the city and counted on your ignorance."

"Ignorance! You insult—"

"I take it back. I just meant they thought they could get away with the trick, and since they didn't they are the stupid ones. Does that satisfy you?"

"What do you do next?"

"I take off the nuts and when I do there is a good chance that the poison-hood will be released and can simply be lifted off."

"It is too dangerous for you to do, the fiends may still have other

84

traps ready when the nut is turned. I will send a strong slave to turn them while we watch from a distance, his death will not matter."

"I'm touched by your concern for my health, but as much as I would like to take advantage of the offer, I cannot. I've been over the same ground and reached the reluctant conclusion that this is one job of work that I have to do myself. Taking off those nuts looks entirely too easy, and that's what makes me suspicious. I'm going to do it and look out for any more trickery at the same time—and that is something that only I can do. Now I suggest you withdraw with the troops to a safer spot."

There was no hesitation about leaving, footsteps rustled quickly on the sand and Jason was alone. The leather walls flapped slackly in the wind and there was no other sound. Jason spat on his palms, controlled a slight shiver and slid into the pit. The wrench fitted neatly over the nut, he wrapped both hands around it and, bracing his leg against the pit wall, began to pull.

And stopped. Three turns of thread on the bolt projected below the nut, scraped clean of metal by the industrious Mikah. Something about them looked very wrong but he didn't know quite what.

"Mikah," he shouted, and had to call loudly two more times before his assistant poked his head tentatively around the screen. "Nip over to the petroleum works and get me one of their bolts threaded with a nut, any size, it doesn't matter."

Jason warmed his hands by the stove until Mikah returned with the oily bolt, then waved him out to rejoin the others. Back in the pit he held it up next to the protruding section of Appsalan bolt and chortled with joy. The threads on the angle bolt were canted at a slightly different angle: where one ran up, the other ran down. The Appsalan threads had been cut in reverse, with a lefthand thread.

Throughout the galaxy there existed as many technical and cultural differences as there were planets, yet one of the few things they all had in common, inherited from their terrestrial ancestors, was a uniformity of thread. Jason had never thought about it before, but when he mentally ran through his experiences on different planets he realized that they were all the same. Screws went into wood, bolts went into threaded holes and nuts all went onto bolts when you turned them with a clockwise motion. Counterclockwise removed them. In his hand was the crude D'zertano nut and bolt, and when he tried it it moved in the same manner. But the engine bolt did not work that way—it had to be turned clockwise to *remove* it.

***

Dropping the nut and bolt he placed the wrench on the massive engine bolt and slowly applied pressure in what felt like the completely wrong direction, as if he were tightening not loosening. It gave slowly, first a quarter then a half turn. And bit by bit the projection threads vanished until they were level with the surface of the nut. It turned easily now and within a minute it fell into the pit—he threw the wrench after it and scrambled out. Standing at the edge he carefully sniffed the air, ready to run at the slightest smell of gas. There was nothing.

The second nut came off as easily as the first and with no ill effects. Jason pushed a sharp chisel between the upper case and the baseplate where he had removed the solder, and when he leaned on it the case shifted slightly, held down only by its own weight.

From the entrance to the enclosure he shouted to the group huddled in the distance. "Come on back—this job is almost finished."

They all took turns at sliding into the pit and looking at the projecting bolts and made appreciative sounds when Jason leaned on the chisel and showed how the case was free.

"There is still the little matter of taking it off," he told them, "and I'm sure that grabbing and heaving is the wrong way. That was my first idea too, but the people who assembled that thing had some bad trouble in store for anyone who tightened those nuts instead of loosening them. Until we find out what that is we are going to tread

86

very lightly. Do you have any big blocks of ice around here, Edipon? It is winter now, isn't it?"

"Ice? Winter?" Edipon mumbled, caught off guard by the change of direction, rubbing abstractedly at the reddened tip of his prominent nose. "Of course it is winter. Ice, there must be ice at the higher lakes in the mountain, they are always frozen at this time of the year. But what do you want ice for?"

"You get it and I'll show you. Have it cut in nice flat blocks that I can stack. I'm not going to lift the hood—I'm going to drop the engine out from underneath it!"

By the time the slaves had brought the ice down from the distant lakes Jason had rigged a strong wooden frame flat on the ground around the engine and pushed sharpened metal wedges under the hood, then had secured the wedges to the frame. Now, if the engine was lowered into the pit, the hood would stay above supported by the wedges. The ice would take care of this. Jason built a foundation of ice under the engine then slipped out the supporting bars. Now as the ice slowly melted the engine would be gently lowered into the pit.

The weather remained cold and the ice refused to melt until Jason had the pit ringed with smoking oil stoves. Water began to run down into the pit and Mikah went to work bailing it out, while the gap between the hood and the baseplate widened. The melting continued for the rest of the day and almost all of the night. Red-eyed and exhausted Jason and Mikah supervised the soggy sinking and when the D'zertanoj returned at dawn the engine rested safely in a pool of mud on the bottom of the pit: the hood was off.

"They're tricky devils over there in Appsala, but Jason dinAlt wasn't born yesterday," he exulted. "Do you see that crock sitting there on top of the engine," he pointed to a sealed container of thick glass the size of a small barrel, filled with an oily greenish liquid; it was clamped down tightly with padded supports. "That's the booby trap. The nuts I took off were on the threaded ends of two bars that held the hood on, but instead of being fastened directly to the hood they were connected by a crossbar that rested on top of that jug. If either nut was tightened instead of being loosened, the bar would have bent and broken the glass. I'll give you exactly one guess as to what would have happened then."

"The poison liquid!"

"None other. And the double-walled hood is filled with it, too. I suggest that as soon as we have dug a deep hole in the desert the hood and container be buried and forgotten about. I doubt if the engine has many other surprises in store, but I'll be careful as I work on it."

"You can fix it? You know what is wrong with it?" Edipon was vibrating with joy.

"Not yet, I have barely looked at the thing. In fact one look was enough to convince that the job will be as easy as stealing *krenoj* from a blind man. The engine is as inefficient and clumsy in construction as your petroleum still. If you people put one tenth of the energy into research and improving your product as you do into hiding it from the competition, you would all be flying jets."

"I forgive your insult because you have done us a service. You will now fix this engine and the other engines. A new day is breaking for us!"

"Right now it is a new night that is breaking for me," Jason yawned. "I have two days sleep to make up. See if you can talk your sons into wiping the water off that engine before it rusts away, and when I get back I'll see what I can do about getting it into running condition."

IX

Edipon's good mood remained and Jason took advantage of it by extracting as many concessions as possible. By hinting that there might be more traps in the engine permission was easily gained to do all the work on the original site instead of inside the sealed and

88

guarded buildings. A covered shed gave them protection from the weather and a test stand was constructed to hold the engines when Jason worked on them. This was of a unique design and built to Jason's exacting specification, and since no one, including Mikah, had ever heard of or seen a test stand before Jason had his way.

The first engine proved to have a burnt-out bearing and Jason rebuilt it by melting down the original bearing metal and casting it in position. When he unbolted the head of the massive single cylinder he shuddered at the clearance around the piston; he could fit his fingers into the opening between the piston and the cylinder wall; by introducing cylinder rings he doubled the compression and power output. When Edipon saw the turn of speed the rebuilt engine gave his *caroj* he hugged Jason to his bosom and promised him the highest reward. This turned out to be a small piece of meat every day to relieve the monotony of the *krenoj* meals, and a doubled guard to make sure that his valuable property did not escape.

Jason had his own plans and kept busy manufacturing a number of pieces of equipment that had nothing at all to do with his engine-overhauling business. While these were being assembled he went about lining up a little aid.

"What would you do if I gave you a club?" he asked a burly slave whom he was helping to haul a log towards his workshop. Narsisi and one of his brothers lazed along out of earshot, bored by the routine of the guard duty.

"What I do with club?" the slave grunted, forehead furrowing and mouth gaping open with the effort of thought.

"That's what I asked. And keep pulling while you think, I don't want the guards to notice anything."

"If I have club, I kill!" the slave announced excitedly, fingers grasping eagerly for coveted weapon.

"Would you kill me?"

"I have club, I kill you, you not so big."

"But if I gave you the club wouldn't I be your friend? Then wouldn't you want to kill someone else?"

The novelty of this alien thought stopped the slave dead and he scratched his head perplexedly until Narsisi lashed him back to work. Jason sighed and found another slave to try his sales program on.

It took a while, but the idea was eventually percolating through the ranks of the slaves. All they had to look forward to from the D'zertanoj was backbreaking labor and an early death. Jason offered them something else, weapons, a chance to kill their masters, and even more killing later when they marched on Appsala. It was difficult for them to grasp the idea that they must work together to accomplish this and not kill Jason and each other as soon as they received weapons.

It was a chancy plan at best, and would probably break down long before any visit could be made to the city. But the revolt should be enough to free them from bondage, even if the slaves fled afterwards. There were less than fifty D'zertanoj at this well station, all men, with their women and children at some other settlement further back in the hills. It would not be too hard to kill them or chase them off and long before they could bring reinforcements Jason and his runaway slaves would be gone. There was just one factor missing from his plans and a new draft of slaves solved even that problem for him.

"Happy days," he laughed, pushing open the door to his quarters and rubbing his hands together with glee. The guard shoved Mikah in after him and locked the door. Jason secured it with his own interior bolt then waved the two others over to the corner farthest from the door and tiny window opening.

***

"New slaves today," he told them, "and one of them is from Appsala, a mercenary or a soldier of some kind that they captured on a skirmish. He knows that they will never let him live long enough to leave here, so he was grateful for any suggestions I had."

"This is man's talk I do not understand," Ijale said, turning away and starting towards the cooking fire.

"You'll understand this," Jason said, taking her by the shoulder. "The soldier knows where Appsala is and can lead us there. The time has come to think about leaving this place."

He had all of her attention now, and Mikah's as well, "How is this?" she gasped.

"I have been making my plans, I have enough files and lockpicks now to crack into every room in this place, a few weapons, the key to the armory and every able bodied slave on my side."

"What do you plan to do?" Mikah asked.

"Stage a servile revolt in the best style. The slaves fight the D'zertanoj and we get away, perhaps with an army helping us, but at least we get away."

"You are talking *revolution*!" Mikah bellowed and Jason jumped him and knocked him to the floor. Ijale held his legs down while Jason squatted on his chest and covered his mouth.

"What is the matter with you? Want to spend the rest of your life rebuilding stolen engines? They are guarding us too well for there to be much chance of our breaking out on our own, so we need allies. We have them ready made, all the slaves."

"Brevilushun...." Mikah mumbled through the restraining fingers.

"Of course it's a revolution. It is also the only possible chance of survival that these poor devils will ever have. Now they are human cattle, beaten and killed on whim. You can't be feeling sorry for the D'zertanoj—every one of them is a murderer ten times over. You've seen them beat people to death. Do you feel that they are too nice to suffer a revolution?"

Mikah relaxed and Jason removed his hand slightly, ready to clamp down if the other's voice rose above a whisper.

"Of course they are not nice, beasts in human garb is more truthful. I feel no mercy for them and they should be wiped out and blotted from the face of the earth as was Sodom and Gomorrah. But it cannot be done by revolution, revolution is evil, inherently evil."

Jason stifled a groan. "Try telling that to two-thirds of the governments that now exist, since that's about how many were founded by revolution. Nice, liberal democratic governments—that were started by a bunch of lads with guns and the immense desire to run things in a manner more beneficial to themselves. How else do you get rid of the powers on your neck if there is no way to legally vote them away? If you can't vote them—shoot them."

"Bloody revolution, it cannot be!"

"All right, no revolution," Jason said, getting up and wiping his hands disgustedly. "We'll change the name. How about calling it a prison break? No, you wouldn't like that either. I have it—liberation! We are going to strike the chains off these poor people and restore them to the lands from which they were stolen. The tiny fact that the slave holders regard them as property and won't think much of the idea, therefore might get hurt in the process, shouldn't bother you. So—will you join me in this Liberation Movement?"

"It is still revolution."

"It is whatever I decide to call it!" Jason raged. "You come along with me on the plans or you will be left behind when we go. You have my word on that." He stomped over and helped himself to some soup and waited for his anger to simmer down.

"I cannot do it ... I cannot do it," Mikah brooded, staring into his rapidly cooling soup as into an oracular crystal ball, seeking guidance there. Jason turned his back in disgust.

***

"Don't end up like him," he warned Ijale, pointing his spoon back over his shoulder. "Not that there is much chance that you ever will coming as you do from a society with its feet firmly planted on the ground, or on the grave to be more accurate. Your people see only concrete facts, and only the most obvious ones, and as simple an abstraction as 'trust' seems beyond you. While this long-faced clown can only think in abstractions of abstractions, and the more unreal they are the better. I bet he even worries about how many angels can dance on the head of a pin."

"I do not worry about it," Mikah broke in, overhearing the remark. "But I do think about it once in a while, it is a problem that cannot be lightly dismissed."

"You see?"

Ijale nodded. "If he is wrong, and I am wrong—then you must be the only one who is right." She nodded in satisfaction at the thought.

"Very nice of you to say so," Jason smiled. "And true, too. I lay no claims to infallibility but I am sure that I can see the difference between abstractions and facts a lot better than either of you, and I am certainly more adroit at handling them. The Jason dinAlt fan club meeting is now adjourned." He reached his hand over his shoulder and patted himself on the back.

"Monster of arrogance," Mikah bellowed.

"Oh, shut up."

"Pride goeth before a fall! You are a maledicent and idolatrous antipietist...."

"Very good."

"... And I grieve that I could have considered aiding you for even a second, or of standing by while you sin, and fear for the weakness of my own soul that I have not been able to resist temptation as I should. It grieves me, but I must do my duty." He banged loudly on the door. "Guard! Guard!"

Jason dropped his bowl and started to scramble to his feet, but slipped in the spilled soup and fell. As he stood again the locks rattled on the door and it opened. If he could reach Mikah before the idiot opened his mouth he would close it forever, or at least knock him out before it was too late.

It was too late. Narsisi poked his head in and blinked sleepily; Mikah struck his most dramatic pose and pointed to Jason. "Seize and arrest that man, I denounce him for attempted revolution, for planning red murder!"

Jason skidded to a halt and back-tracked, diving into a bag of his personal belongings that lay against the wall. He scrabbled in it, then kicked the contents about and finally came up with a metal-forming hammer that had a weighty solid lead head.

"More traitor you," Jason shouted at Mikah as he ran at Narsisi who had been dumbly watching the performance and mulling over Mikah's words. Slow as he appeared, there was nothing wrong with his reflexes and his shield snapped up and took Jason's blow while his club spun over neatly and rapped Jason on the back of the hand: the numbed fingers opened and the hammer dropped to the floor.

"I think you two better come with me, my father will know what to do," he said, pushing Jason and Mikah ahead of him out the door. He locked it and called for one of his brothers to stand guard, then poked his captives down the hall. They shuffled along in their leg-irons, Mikah nobly as a martyr and Jason seething and grinding his teeth.

Edipon was not at all stupid when it came to slave rebellions, and sized up the situation even faster than Narsisi could relate it.

"I have been expecting this, so it comes as no surprise." His eyes held a mean little glitter when he leveled them at Jason. "I knew the time would come when you would try to overthrow me, which was why I permitted this other to assist you and to learn your skills. As I expected he has betrayed you to gain your position, which I award him now."

"Betray? I did this for no personal gain," Mikah protested.

"Only the purest of motives," Jason laughed coldly. "Don't believe a word this pious crook tells you, Edipon. I'm not planning any revolutions, he just said that to get my job."

"You caluminate me, Jason! I never lie—you are planning revolt. You told me—"

"Silence both of you, or I'll have you beaten to death. This is my judgment. The slave Mikah has betrayed the slave Jason, and whether the slave Jason is planning rebellion or not is completely unimportant. His assistant would have not denounced him unless he was sure that he could do the work as well, which is the only fact that has any importance to me. Your ideas about a worker-class have troubled me Jason. I will be glad to kill them and you at the same time. Chain him with the slaves. Mikah, I award you Jason's quarter and woman, and as long as you do the work well I will not kill you. Do it a long time and you will live a long time.

"Only the purest of motives, is that what you said, Mikah?" Jason shouted back as he was kicked from the room.

***

The descent from the pinnacle of power was fast and smooth. Within half an hour new shackles were on Jason's wrists and he was chained to the wall in a dark room filled with other slaves. His leg-irons had been left on as an additional reminder of his new status. He rattled the chains and examined them in the dim light of a distant lamp as soon as the door was closed.

"How comes the revolution?" the slave chained next to him leaned over and asked in a hoarse whisper.

"Very funny, ha-ha," Jason grumbled, then moved closer for a better look at the man who had a fine case of strabismus, his eyes pointing in independent directions. "You look familiar ... are you the new slave I talked to today?"

"That's me, Snarbi, fine soldier, pikeman, checked out on club and dagger, seven kills and two possibles on my record, you can check it yourself at the guild hall."

"I remember it all Snarbi, including the fact that you know your way back to Appsala."

"I've been around."

"Then the revolution is still on, in fact it is starting right now but I want to keep it small. Instead of freeing all these slaves what do you say to the idea that we two escape by ourselves?"

"Best idea I heard since torture was invented, we don't need all these stupid people. They just get in the way. Keep the operation small and fast, that's what I always say."

"I always say that, too," Jason agreed, digging into his boot with his fingertip. He had managed to shove his best file and a lockpick into hiding there while Mikah was betraying him back in their room. The attack on Narsisi with the hammer had just been a cover up.

Jason had made the file himself after many attempts at manufacturing and hardening steel, and the experiments had been successful. He picked out the clay that covered the cut he had made in his leg-cuffs and tackled the soft iron with vigor; within three minutes they were lying on the floor.

"You a magician?" Snarbi whispered, shuddering back.

"Mechanic. On this planet they're the same thing." He looked around but the exhausted slaves were all asleep and had heard nothing. Wrapping a piece of leather around it to muffle the sound he began to file a link in the chain that secured the shackles on his wrists. "Snarbi," he asked, "are we on the same chain?"

"Yeah, the chain goes through these iron cuff things and holds the whole row of slaves together, the other end goes out through a hole in the wall."

"Couldn't be better. I'm filing one of these links, and when it goes we're both free. See if you can't slip the chain through the holes in your shackles and lay it down without letting the next slave know what is happening. We'll wear these iron cuffs for now, there is no time to play around with them and they shouldn't bother us too much. Do the guards come through here at all during the night to check on the slaves?"

"Not since I've been here, just wake us up in the morning by pulling on the chain."

"Then let's hope that's what happens again tonight, because we are going to need plenty of time—*there!*" The file had cut through the link. "See if you can get enough of a grip on the other end of this link while I hold this end, we'll try and bend it open a bit." They strained silently until the opening gaped wide and the next link fitted through the cut.

They slipped the chain and laid it silently on the ground, then drifted noiselessly to the door.

"Is there a guard outside?" Jason asked.

"Not that I know. I don't think they have enough men here to guard all the slaves."

The door would not budge when they pushed against it, and there was just light enough to make out the large keyhole of a massive inset lock. Jason probed lightly with the pick and curled his lip in contempt.

"These idiots have left the key in the lock." He pulled off the stiffest of his leather wrappings and after flattening it out pushed it under the badly fitting bottom edge of the door, leaving just a bit to hold onto. Then he poked lightly at the key through the keyhole and heard it thud to the ground outside. When he pulled the leather back in the key was lying in the center of it. The door unlocked silently and a moment later they were outside, staring tensely into the darkness.

"Let's go! Run, get away from here," Snarbi said and Jason grabbed him by the throat and pulled him back.

"Isn't there one drop of constructive intelligence on this planet? How are you going to get to Appsala without food or water, and if you find some—how can you carry enough? You want to stay alive follow my instructions. I'm going to lock this door first so that no one stumbles onto our escape by accident. Then we are going to get some transport and leave here in style. Agreed?"

The answer was only a choked rattle until Jason opened his fingers a bit and let some air into the man's lungs. A labored groan must have meant assent because Snarbi tottered after him when he made his way through the dark alleys between the buildings.

Getting clear of the walled refinery town presented no problem since the few sentries were only looking for trouble from the outside. It was equally easy to approach Jason's leather-walled worksite from the rear and slip through it at the spot where Jason had cut the leather and sewn up the opening with thin twine.

"Sit here and touch nothing or you will be cursed for life," he commanded the shivering Snarbi, then slipped towards the front entrance with a small sledge hammer clutched in his fist. He was pleased to see one of Edipon's other sons on guard duty, leaning against a pole and dozing. Jason gently lifted his leather helm with his free hand and tapped once with the hammer: the guard slept even more soundly.

"Now we can get to work," Jason said when he had returned inside, and clicked a firelighter to the wick of a lantern.

"What are you doing? They'll see us, kill us—escaped slaves."

"Stick with me Snarbi and you'll be wearing shoes. Lights here can't be seen by the sentries, I made sure of that when I sited the place. And we have a piece of work to do before we leave—we have to build a *caroj*."

They did not have to build it from scratch, but there was enough truth in the statement to justify it. His most recently rebuilt and most powerful engine was still bolted to the test stand, a fact that justified all the night's risks. Three *caroj* wheels lay among the other debris of the camp and two of them were to be bolted to the engine while it was still on the stand. The ends of the driving axle cleared the edges of the stand, Jason threaded the securing wheel bolts into place and utilized Snarbi to tighten them.

At the other end of the stand was a strong, swiveling post that had been a support for his test instruments, and seemed strangely large for this small task. It was. When the instruments were stripped away a single bar remained projecting backwards like a tiller handle. When a third wheel was fitted with a stub axle and slid into place in the forked lower end of the post the test stand looked remarkably like a three-wheeled, steerable, steam engine powered platform that was mounted on legs. This is exactly what it was, what Jason had designed it to be from the first, and the supporting legs came away with the same ease that the other parts had been attached. Escape had always taken first priority in his plans.

Snarbi dragged over the crockery jars of oil, water and fuel while Jason filled the tanks. He started the fire under the boiler and loaded aboard tools and the small supply of *krenoj* he had managed to set aside from their rations. All of this took time, but not time enough. It would soon be dawn and they would have to leave before then, and he could no longer avoid making up his mind. He could not leave Ijale here, and if he went to get her he could not refuse to take Mikah as well. The man had saved his life, no matter what murderous idiocies he had managed to pull since that time. Jason believed that you owed something to a man who prolonged your existence, but he also wondered just how much he still owed. In Mikah's case he felt the balance of the debt to be mighty small, if not overdrawn. Perhaps this one last time.

"Keep an eye on the engine and I'll be back as soon as I can," he said, jumping to the ground and loading on equipment.

"You want me to do *what*? Stay here with this devil machine? I cannot! It will burn and consume me—"

"Act your age, Snarbi, your physical age if not your mental one. This rolling junk pile was made by men and repaired and improved by me, no demons involved. It burns oil to make heat that makes steam that goes to this tube to push that rod to make those wheels go around so we can move, and that is as much of the theory of the steam engine as you are going to get from me. Maybe you can understand this better—only I can get you safely away from here. Therefore, you will stay and do as I say or I will beat your brains in. Clear?"

Snarbi nodded dumbly.

"Fine. All you have to do is sit here and look at this little green disk, see it? If it should pop out before I come back turn *this* handle in *this* direction. Clear enough? That way the safety valve won't blow and wake the whole country and we'll still have a head of steam."

Jason went out past the still-silent sentry and headed back towards the refinery station. Instead of a club or a dagger he was armed with a well tempered broadsword that he had managed to manufacture under the noses of the guards. They had examined everything he brought from the worksite, since he had been working in the evenings in his room, but ignored everything he manufactured as being beyond their comprehension. This primordial mental attitude had been of immense value for in addition to the sword he carried a sack of molotails, a simple weapon of assault whose origins were lost in pre-history. Small crocks were filled with the most combustible of the refinery's fractions and wrapped around outside with cloth that he had soaked in the same liquid. The stench made him dizzy and he hoped that they would repay his efforts when the time came, since they were completely untried. In use one lit the outer covering and threw them. The crockery burst on impact and the fuse ignited the contents. Theoretically.

Getting back in proved to be as easy as getting out, and Jason felt an unmistakable twinge of regret. His subconscious had obviously been hoping that there would be a disturbance and he would have to retreat to save himself, his subconscious obviously being very short on interest in saving the slave girl and his nemesis, particularly at the risk of his own skin. His subconscious was disappointed. He was in the building where his quarters lay, trying to peek around the corner to see if a guard was at the door. There was, and he seemed to be dozing, but something jerked him awake. He had heard nothing but he sniffed the air and wrinkled his nose; the powerful smell of water-of-power from Jason's molotails had roused him and he spotted Jason before he could pull back.

"Who is there?" he shouted and advanced at a lumbering run.

There was no quiet way out of this one so Jason leaped out with an echoing shout and lunged. The blade went right under the man's guard—he must never have seen a sword before—and the tip caught him full in the throat. He expired with a bubbling wail that stirred voices deeper in the building. Jason sprang over the corpse and tore at the multifold bolts and locks that sealed the door. Footsteps were running in the distance when he finally threw the door open and ran in.

"Get out and quick we're escaping!" he shouted at them and pushed the dazed Ijale towards the door and exacted a great deal of pleasure from landing a tremendous kick that literally lifted Mikah through the opening, where he collided with Edipon who had just run up waving a club. Jason leaped over the tumbled forms, rapped Edipon behind the ear with the hilt of his sword and dragged Mikah to his feet.

"Get out to the engine works," he ordered his still uncomprehending companions. "I have a *caroj* there that we can get away in." He cursed them and they finally broke into clumsy motion. There were shouts from behind him and an armed mob of D'zertanoj ran into view. Jason pulled down the hall light, burning his hand on the hot base at the same time, and applied its open flame to one of his molotails. The wick caught with a roar of flame and he threw it at approaching soldiers before it could burn his hand. It flew towards them, hit the wall and broke, inflammable fuel spurted in every direction and the flame went out.

Jason cursed and grappled for another molotail, because if they didn't work he was dead. The D'zertanoj had hesitated a moment rather than walk through the puddle of spilled water-of-power and in that instant he hurled the second fire bomb. This one burst nicely too, and lived up to its maker's expectations when it ignited the first molotail as well and the passageway filled with a curtain of fire. Holding his hand around the lamp flame so it wouldn't go out, Jason ran after the others.

So far the alarm had not spread outside of the building and Jason bolted the door from the outside. By the time this was broken open and the confusion sorted out they would be clear of the buildings. There was no need for the lamp now and would only give him away. He blew it out and from the desert came a continuous and ear-piercing scream.

"He's done it," Jason groaned. "That's the safety valve on the steam engine!"

He bumped into Ijale and Mikah who were milling about confusedly in the dark, kicked Mikah again out of sheer malice and hatred of all mankind, and led them towards the worksite at a dead run.

***

They escaped unharmed mainly because of the confusion on all sides of them. The D'zertanoj seemed to never have experienced a night attack before, which they apparently thought this was, and did an incredible amount of rushing about and shouting. Matters were not helped by the burning building nor the unconscious form of Edipon that was carried from the blaze. All the D'zertanoj had been roused by the scream of the safety valve, that was still bleeding irreplacable steam into the night air, and there was much milling about.

In the confusion the fleeing slaves were not noticed, and Jason led them around the guard post on the walls and directly towards the worksite. They were spotted as they crossed the empty ground and after some hesitation the guard ran in pursuit. Jason was leading the enemy directly to his precious steam-wagon, but he had no choice. The thing was certainly making its presence known in any case, and unless he reached it at once the head of steam would be gone and they would be trapped. He leaped the still recumbent guard at the entrance and ran towards his machine. Snarbi was cowering behind one wheel but there was no time to give him any attention. As Jason jumped onto the platform the safety valve closed and the sudden stillness was frightening. The steam was gone.

With frantic grabs he spun valves and shot one glance at the indicator: there wasn't enough steam left to roll the meters. Water gurgled and the boiler hissed and clacked at him while screams of anger came from the D'zertanoj as they ran into the enclosure and saw the bootleg *caroj*. Jason thrust the end of a molotail into the firebox; it caught fire and he turned and hurled it at them. The angry cries turned into screams of fear as the tongues of flame licked up at the pursuers and they retreated in disorder. Jason ran after them and hastened their departure with another molotail. They seemed to be retreating as far as the refinery walls, but he could not be sure in the darkness if some of them weren't creeping around to the sides.

He hurried back to the *caroj*, tapped on the still-unmoving pressure indicator and opened the fuel feed wide. As an afterthought he wired down the safety valve since his reinforced boiler should hold more pressure than the valve had been originally adjusted for. Once this was finished he chewed at his oily fingernails since there was nothing else that could be done until the pressure built up again. The D'zertanoj would rally, someone would take charge, and they would attack the worksite. If they had enough steam before this happened, they would escape. If not—

"Mikah, and you, too, you cowering slob Snarbi you, get behind this thing and push," Jason said.

"What has happened," Mikah asked. "Have you started this revolution? If so I will give no aid...."

"We're escaping, if that's all right with you. Just I, Ijale and a guide to show us the way. You don't have to come—"

"I will join you. There is nothing criminal in escaping from these barbarians."

"Very nice of you to say so. Now push. I want this steamobile in the center, far from all the walls, and pointing towards the desert. Down the valley I guess, is that right, Snarbi?"

"Down the valley, sure, that's the way." His voice was still rasping from the earlier throttling, Jason was pleased to notice.

"Stop it here and everyone aboard. Grab onto those bars I've bolted along the sides so you won't get bounced off, if we ever start moving that is."

Jason took a quick look through his workshop to make sure everything they might need was already loaded, then reluctantly climbed aboard himself. He blew out the lantern and they sat there in the darkness, their faces lit from below by the flickering glow from the firebox, while the tension mounted. There was no way to measure time since each second took an eternity to drag by.

The walls of the worksite cut off any view of the outside and within a few moments imagination had peopled the night with silent hordes creeping towards them, huddling about the thin barrier of leather, ready to swoop down and crush them in an instant.

"Let's run for it," Snarbi gurgled and tried to jump from the platform. "We're trapped here, we'll never get away...."

Jason tripped him and knocked him flat, then pounded his head against the floor planks a few times until he quieted.

"I can sympathize with that poor man," Mikah said severely. "You are a brute, Jason, to punish him for his natural feelings. Cease your sadistic attack and join me in a prayer."

"If this poor man you are so sorry for had simply done his duty and watched the boiler, we would all be safely away from here by now. And if you have enough breath for a prayer, put it to better use by blowing into the firebox. It's not going to be wishes or prayers that gets us out of here, just a head of steam."

***

A howled battlecry was echoed by massed voices and a squad of D'zertanoj burst in through the entrance, and at the same instant the rear of the leather wall went down and more armed men swarmed over it. The immobile *caroj* was trapped between the two groups of attackers who laughed happily as they charged. Jason cursed and lit four molotails at the same time and hurled them two and two in opposite directions. Before they hit he had jumped to the steam valve and wound it open; with a hissing clank the *caroj* shuddered and got underway.

For the moment the attackers were held back by the walls of flame and screamed even louder as the machine moved away at right angles from between their two groups. The air whistled with crossbow bolts, but most were badly aimed and only a few thudded into the baggage. With each revolution of the wheels their speed picked up and when they hit the walls the hides parted with a creaking snap. Strips of leather whipped at them, then they were through.

The shouts and the fires grew dimmer behind them as they streaked down the valley at a suicidal pace, hissing, rattling and crashing over the bumps. Jason clung to the tiller and shouted for Mikah to come relieve him, since if he let go of the thing they would turn and crash in an instant, and as long as he held it he couldn't cut down the steam. Some of this finally penetrated to Mikah because he crawled forward grasping desperately to every hand-hold until he crouched beside Jason.

"Grab this tiller and hold it straight and steer around anything big enough to see."

As soon as the steering was taken over Jason worked his way back

105

to the engine and throttled down; they slowed to a clanking walk then stopped completely. Ijale moaned and Jason felt as if every inch of his body had been beaten with hammers. There was no sign of pursuit since it would be at least an hour before they could raise steam in the *caroj* and no one on foot could have possibly matched their headlong pace. The lantern he had used earlier had vanished during the wild ride so Jason dug out another one of his own construction.

"On your feet, Snarbi," he ordered. "I've cracked us all out of slavery so now it is time for you to do some of the guiding that you were telling me about. Walk ahead with this light and pick out a nice smooth track going in the right direction. I never did have a chance to build headlights for this machine so you will have to do instead."

Snarbi climbed down unsteadily and walked out in front. Jason opened the valve a bit and they clattered forward on his trail as Mikah turned the tiller to follow. Ijale crawled over and settled herself against Jason's side, shivering with cold and fright. He patted her shoulder.

"Relax," he said, "from now on this is just a pleasure trip."

X

They were six days out of Putl'ko and their supplies were almost exhausted. The country, once they were away from the mountains, became more fertile, an undulating pampas of grass with enough streams and herds of beasts to assure that they did not starve. It was fuel that mattered, and that afternoon Jason had opened their last jar. They stopped a few hours before dark since their fresh meat was gone, and Snarbi took the crossbow and went out to shoot something for the pot. Since he was the only one who could handle the clumsy weapon with any kind of skill in spite of his ocular deficiencies, and who knew about the local game, this task had been assigned to him. With longer contact his fear of the *caroj* had lessened, and his self-esteem rose at his recognized ability as a

106

hunter. He strolled arrogantly out into the knee-high grass, crossbow over his shoulder, whistling tunelessly through his teeth. Jason stared after him and once again felt a growing unease.

"I don't trust that wall-eyed mercenary, I don't trust him for one second," he muttered.

"Were you talking to me?" Mikah asked.

"I wasn't but I might as well now. Have you noticed anything interesting about the country we have been passing through, anything different?"

"Nothing. It is a wilderness, untouched by the hand of man."

"Then you must be blind, because I have been seeing things the last two days, and I know just as little about woodcraft as you do. Ijale," he called, and she looked up from the boiler over which she was heating a thin stew of their last *krenoj*. "Leave that stuff, it tastes just as bad whatever is done to it, and if Snarbi has any luck we'll be having roast in any case. Tell me, have you seen anything strange or different about the land we passed through today."

"Nothing strange, just signs of people. Twice we passed places where the grass was flat and branches broken as if a *caroj* passed two or three days ago, maybe more. And once there was a place where someone had built a cooking fire, but that was very old."

"Nothing to be seen, Mikah?" Jason asked with raised eyebrows. "See what a lifetime of *krenoj* hunting can do for the sense of observation and terrain."

"I am no savage. You cannot expect me to look out for that sort of thing."

"I don't. I have learned to expect very little from you beside trouble. Only now I am going to need your help. This is Snarbi's last night of freedom whether he knows it or not, and I don't want him standing guard tonight, so you and I will split the shift."

Mikah was astonished. "I do not understand. What do you mean this is his last night of freedom?"

"It should be obvious by now—even to you—after seeing how the social ethic works on this planet. What did you think we were going to do when we came to Appsala—follow Snarbi like sheep to the slaughter? I have no idea what he is planning. I just know he must be planning something. When I ask him about the city he only answers in generalities. Of course he is a hired mercenary who wouldn't know too much of the details, but he must know a lot more than he is telling us. He says we are still four days away from the city. My guess is that we are no more than one or two. In the morning I intend to grab him and tie him up, then swing over to those hills there and find a place to hole up. I'll fix some chains for Snarbi so he can't get away, then I'll do a scout of the city...."

"You are going to chain this poor man, make a slave of him for no reason!"

"I'm not going to make a slave of him, just chain him to make sure he doesn't lead us into some trap that will benefit him. This souped-up *caroj* is valuable enough to tempt any of the locals, and if he can sell me as an engine-mechanic slave his fortune is made."

***

"I will not hear this!" Mikah stormed. "You condemn the man on no evidence at all, just because of your nasty minded suspicions. Judge not lest ye be judged yourself! And you play the hypocrite as well, because I well remember your telling me that a man is innocent until proven guilty."

"Well this man is guilty, if you want to put it that way, guilty of being a member of this broken down society, which means that he will always act in certain ways at certain times. Haven't you learned anything about these people yet? Ijale!" She looked up from contented munching on a *krenoj*, obviously not listening to the argument. "Tell me, what is your opinion? We are coming soon to a place where Snarbi has friends, or people who will help him. What do you think he will do?"

"Say hello to the people he knows? Maybe they will give him a *krenoj*." She smiled in satisfaction at her answer and took another bite.

"That's not quite what I had in mind," Jason said patiently. "What if we three are with him when we come to the people, and the people see us and the *caroj*...."

She sat up, alarmed. "We can't go with him! If he has people there they will fight us, make us slaves, take the *caroj*. You must kill Snarbi at once."

"Bloodthirsty heathen...." Mikah began in his best denunciatory voice, but quit when he saw Jason pick up a heavy hammer.

"Do you understand yet?" Jason asked. "By tying up Snarbi I'm only conforming to a local code of ethic, like saluting in the army or not eating with your fingers in polite society. In fact I'm being a little slipshod, since by local custom I should kill him before he can make us trouble."

"It cannot be, I cannot believe it. You cannot judge and condemn a man upon such flimsy evidence."

"I'm not condemning him," Jason said with growing irritation, "Just making sure that he can't cause me any trouble. You don't have to agree with me to help me, just don't get in my way. And split the guard with me tonight. Whatever I do in the morning will be on my shoulders and no concern of yours."

"He is returning," Ijale hissed, and a moment later Snarbi came up through the high grass.

"Got a *cervo*," he announced proudly, and dropped the animal down before them. "Cut him up, makes good chops and roast. We eat tonight."

He was completely innocent and without guile and the only thing guilty about him was his shifty gaze which could be blamed completely on his crossed eyes. Jason wondered for a second if his assessment of the danger was correct, then remembered where he was and lost his doubts. Snarbi would be committing no crime if he tried to kill or enslave them, just doing what any ordinary, decent slave-holding barbarian would do in his place. Jason searched through his tool box for some rivets that could be used to fasten the leg irons on the man.

They had a filling dinner and the others turned in at dusk and were quickly asleep. Jason, tired from the labors of the trip and heavy with food, forced himself to remain awake, trying to keep alert for trouble both from within and from without. When he became too sleepy he paced around the camp until the cold drove him back to the shelter of the still-warm boiler. Above him the stars wheeled slowly and when a prominent one reached the zenith he estimated it was midnight, or a bit after. He shook Mikah awake.

"You're on now. Keep your eyes and ears open for anything stirring and don't forget a careful watch there," he jerked his thumb at Snarbi's silent form. "Wake me up at once if there's anything suspicious."

***

Sleep dropped like a heavy curtain and Jason barely stirred until the first light of dawn touched the sky. Only the brighter stars were visible on the eastern horizon and he could see a ground fog rising from the grass around them. Near him were the huddled forms of the two sleepers and the farthest one shifted in his sleep and he realized it was Mikah.

Sleep fell away instantly and he bounded out of his skin covers and grabbed the other man by the shoulders. "What are you doing asleep?" he raged. "You were supposed to be on guard."

Mikah opened his eyes and blinked. "I was on guard, but towards morning Snarbi awoke and offered to take his turn. I could not refuse him...."

"You couldn't WHAT? After what I said—"

"That was why. I could not judge an innocent man guilty and be a party to your unfair action. Therefore, I left him on guard."

"You did, did you?" Jason grated with rage and pulled an unfelt handful of hair from his newgrown beard. "Then where is he? Do you see anyone on guard?"

Mikah looked in a careful circle and saw only the two of them and the wakening Ijale. "He seems to have gone. He has proven his untrustworthiness and in the future we will not allow him to stand guard."

Jason raged, drew his foot back for a kick in the local reflex then realized he had no time for such indulgences and dived for the steamobile. The firelighter worked at the first shot, for a rare change, and he lit the boiler. It roared merrily but when he tapped the indicator he saw the fuel was almost gone. There would be enough left in the last jug to take them to safety before whatever trouble Snarbi was planning arrived. But the jug was gone.

"That tears it," Jason said resignedly after a hectic search of the *caroj* and the surrounding plain. The water-of-power had vanished with Snarbi who, afraid as he was of the steam engine, apparently knew enough from observing Jason fueling the thing that it could not move without the vital liquid. An empty feeling of resignation had replaced Jason's first rage: he should have known better than to trust Mikah with anything, particularly when it involved an ethical point. He stared at the man, now calmly eating a bit of cold roast and marveled at the unruffled calm. "This doesn't bother you, the fact that you have condemned us all to slavery again?"

"I did what was right, I had no other choice. We must live as moral creatures or sink to the level of the animals."

"But when you live with people who behave like animals—how do you survive?

"You live as they do—as you do, Jason," he said with majestic judgment, "twisting and turning with fear and unable to avoid your fate no matter how you squirm. Or you live as I have done, as a man of conviction, knowing what is right and not letting your head be turned by the petty needs of the day. And if one lives this way one can die happy."

"Then die happy!" Jason snarled and reached for his sword, but settled back again glumly before he picked it up. "To think that I ever thought I could teach you anything about the reality of existence here when you have never experienced reality before nor ever will until the day you die. You carry your own attitudes, which are your reality, around with you all the time, and they are more solid to you than this ground we are sitting upon."

"For once we are in agreement, Jason. I have tried to open your eyes to the true light, but you turn away and will not see. You ignore the Eternal Law for the exigencies of the moment and are, therefore, damned."

The pressure indicator on the boiler hissed and popped out, but the fuel level was at the absolute bottom.

"Grab some food for breakfast, Ijale," Jason said, "and get away from this machine. The fuel is gone and it's finished."

"I shall make a bundle to carry, we will escape on foot."

"No, that's out of the question. Snarbi knows this country and he knew we would find out that he was missing at dawn. Whatever kind of trouble he is bringing is already on the way and we wouldn't be able to escape on foot. So we might as well save our energy. But they aren't getting my handmade, super-charged steamobile!" he added with sudden vehemence, grabbing up the crossbow. "Back both of you, far back. They'll make a slave of me for my talents, but no free samples go with it. If they want one of these hot-rod steam wagons, they are going to have to pay for it!"

Jason lay down flat at the maximum range of the crossbow and his third quarrel hit the boiler. It went up with a most satisfactory bang

and small pieces of metal and wood rained down all around. In the
distance he heard shouting and the barking of dogs.

***

When he stood he could see a distant line of
men advancing through the tall grass and
when they were closer large dogs were also
visible, tugging at their leashes. Though they
must have come far in a few hours they
approached at a steady trot, experienced
runners, in thin leather garments each
carrying a short, laminated bow and a full
quiver of arrows. They swooped up in a
semicircle, their great hounds slavering to be
loosed, and stopped when the three strangers
were within bow range. They notched their
arrows and waited with alert patience, staying
well clear of the smoking ruins of the caroj,
until Snarbi finally staggered up half supported by two other
runners.

"You now belong to ... the Hertug Persson ... and are his slaves....
What happened to the *caroj*?" He screamed this last when he
spotted the smoking wreck and would have collapsed except for the
sustaining arms. Evidently the new slaves decreased in value with
the loss of the machine. He stumbled over to it and, when none of
the soldiers would help him, gathered up what he could find of
Jason's artifacts and tools. When he had bundled them up, and the
foot cavalry had seen that he suffered no injury from the contact,
they reluctantly agreed to carry them. One of the soldiers, identical
in dress with the others, seemed to be in charge, and when he
signaled a return they closed in on the three prisoners and nudged
them to their feet with drawn bows.

"I'm coming, I'm coming," Jason said, gnawing on a bone, "but I'm
going to finish my breakfast first. I see an endless vista
of *krenoj* stretching out before me and intend to enjoy this last meal
before entering servitude."

113

The lead soldiers looked confused and turned to their officer for orders. "Who is this?" he asked Snarbi, pointing at the still seated Jason. "Is there any reason why I should not kill him."

"You can't!" Snarbi choked, and turned a dirty shade of white. "He is the one who built the devil-wagon and knows all of its secrets. Hertug Persson will torture him to build another."

Jason wiped his fingers on the grass and reluctantly stood. "All right gentlemen, let's go. And on the way perhaps someone can tell me just who Hertug Persson is and what is going to happen next."

"I'll tell you," Snarbi bragged as they started the march. "He is Hertug of the Perssonoj. I have fought for the Perssonoj and they knew me and I saw the Hertug himself and he believed me. The Perssonoj are very powerful in Appsala and have many powerful secrets, but not as powerful as the Trozelligoj who have the secret of the *caroj* and the *jetilo*. I knew I could ask any price of the Perssonoj if I brought them the secret of the *caroj*. And I will." He trust his face close to Jason's with a fierce grimace. "You will tell them the secret. I will help them torture you until you tell."

Jason put out his toe as they walked and Snarbi tripped over it and when the traitor fell he walked the length of his body. None of the soldiers paid any attention to this exchange and when they had passed Snarbi staggered to his feet and tottered after them shouting curses. Jason did not hear them, he had troubles enough as it was.

XI

Seen from the surrounding hills, Appsala looked like a burning city that was being slowly washed into the sea. Only when they had come closer was it clear that the smoke was from the multifold chimneys, both large and small, that studded the buildings, and that the city began at the shore and covered a number of islands in what must be a shallow lagoon. Large sea-going ships were tied up at the seaward side of the city and closer to the mainland smaller craft were being poled through the canals. Jason searched anxiously for a spaceport or any signs of interstellar culture but saw nothing. Then the hills intervened as the trail cut off to one side and approached the sea some distance from the city.

A fair-sized sailing vessel was tied up at the end of a stone wharf, obviously awaiting them, and the captives were tied hand and foot and tossed into the hold. Jason managed to wriggle around until he could get his eye to a crack between two badly fitting planks and recited a running travelogue of the cruise, apparently for the edification of his companions, but really for his own benefit since the sound of his own voice always cheered and encouraged him.

"Our voyage is nearing its close and before us opens up the romantic and ancient city of Appsala, famed for its loathsome customs, murderous natives and archaic sanitation facilities, of which this watery channel this ship is now entering seems to be the major cloaca. There are islands on both sides, the smaller ones covered with hovels so decrepit that in comparison the holes in the ground of the humblest animals appear to be palaces, while the larger islands appear to be forts, each one walled and barbicaned and presenting a warlike face to the world. There couldn't be that many forts in a town this size so I am led to believe that each one is undoubtedly the guarded stronghold of one of the tribes, groups or clans that our friend Judas told us about. Look on these monuments to ultimate selfishness and beware: this is the end product of the system that begins with slave-holders like the former Ch'aka with their tribes of *krenoj* crackers, and builds up through familiar hierarchies like the D'zertanoj and reaches its zenith of depravity behind those strong walls. It is still absolute power that rules absolutely, each man out for all that he can get and the only way to climb being over the bodies of others, and all physical discoveries and inventions being treated as private and personal secrets to be hidden and used only for personal gain. Never have I seen human greed and selfishness carried to such extremes and I admire Homo sapiens' capacity to follow through on an idea, no matter how it hurts."

The ship lost way as it backed its sails and Jason fell from his precarious perch into the stinking bilge. "The descent of man," he muttered and inched his way out.

Piles grated along the sides and with much shouting and cursed orders the ship came to a halt. The hatch above was slid back and the three captives were rushed to the deck. The ship was tied up to a dock in a pool of water surrounded by buildings and high walls. Behind them a large sea gate was just swinging shut, through which the ship had entered from the canal. They could see no more because they were pushed into a doorway and through halls and past guards until they ended up in a large central room. It was unfurnished except for the dais at the far end on which stood a large and rusty iron throne. The man on the throne, undoubtedly the Hertug Persson, sported a magnificent white beard and shoulder length hair, his nose was round and red, his eyes blue and watery. He nibbled at a *krenoj* impaled delicately on a two-tined iron fork.

***

"Tell me," the Hertug shouted suddenly, "why you should not be killed at once?"

"We are your slaves, Hertug, we are your slaves," everyone in the room shouted in unison, waving their hands in the air at the same time. Jason missed the first chorus, but came in on the second. Only Mikah did not join in the chant-and-wave, speaking instead in a solitary voice after the pledge of allegiance was completed.

"I am no man's slave."

The commander of the soldiers swung his thick bow in a short arc that terminated on the top of Mikah's head: he dropped stunned to the floor.

"You have a new slave, oh Hertug," the commander said.

"Which is the one who knows the secrets of the *caroj*?" the Hertug asked and Snarbi pointed at Jason.

"Him there, oh mightiness. He can make *caroj* and he can make the

116

monster that burns and moves them, I know because I watched him do it. He also made balls of fire that burned the D'zertanoj and many other things. I brought him to be your slave so that he could make *caroj* for the Perssonoj. Here are the pieces of the *caroj* we traveled in, after it was consumed by its own fire." Snarbi shook the tools and burnt fragments out onto the floor and the Hertug curled his lip at them.

"What proof is this?" he asked, and turned to Jason. "These things mean nothing. How can you prove to me, slave, that you can do the things he says?"

Jason entertained briefly the idea to deny all knowledge of the matter, which would be a neat revenge against Snarbi who would certainly meet a sticky end for causing all this trouble for nothing, but he discarded the thought as fast as it came. Partly for humanitarian reasons, Snarbi could not help being what he was, but mostly because he had no particular desire to be put to the question. He knew nothing about the local torture methods, and he wanted to keep it that way.

"Proof is easy, Hertug of all the Perssonoj, because I know everything about everything. I can build machines that walk, that talk, that run, fly, swim, bark like a dog and roll on their backs."

"You will build a *caroj* for me?"

"It could be arranged, if you have the right kind of tools I could use. But I must first know what is the specialty of your clan, if you know what I mean. Like the Trozelligoj make *caroj* and the D'zertanoj pump oil. What do your people do?"

"You cannot know as much as you say if you do not know of the glories of the Perssonoj!"

"I come from a distant land and as you know news travels slowly around these parts."

"Not around the Perssonoj," the Hertug said scornfully and thumped his chest. "We can talk across the width of the country and always know where our enemies are. We can send magic on wires to kill, or magic to make light in a glass ball or magic that will pluck the sword from an enemy's hand and drive terror into his heart."

"It sounds like your gang has the monopoly on electricity, which is good to hear. If you have some heavy forging equipment...."

"Stop!" the Hertug ordered. "Leave! Out—everyone except the *sciuloj*. Not the new slave, he stays here," he shouted when the soldiers grabbed Jason.

***

The room emptied and the handful of men who remained were all a little long in the tooth and each wore a brazen, sun-burst type decoration on his chest. They were undoubtedly adept in the secret electrical arts and they fingered their weapons and grumbled with unconcealed anger at Jason's forbidden knowledge. The Hertug signaled him to continue.

"You used a sacred word. Who told it to you? Speak quickly or you will be killed."

"Didn't I tell you I knew everything? I can build a *caroj* and given a little time I can improve on your electrical works, if your technology is on the same level as the rest of this planet."

"Do you know what lies behind the forbidden portal?" the Hertug asked, pointing to a barred, locked and guarded door at the other end of the room. "There is no way you can have seen what is there, but if you can tell me what lies beyond it I will know you are the wizard that you claim you are."

"I have a very strange feeling that I have been over this ground once before," Jason sighed. "All right, here goes. You people here make electricity, maybe chemically, though I doubt if you would get enough power that way, so you must have a generator of some sort. That will be a big magnet, a piece of special iron that can pick up other iron, and you spin it around fast next to some coils of wire and out comes electricity. You pipe this through copper wire to whatever

118

devices you have, and they can't be very many. You say you talk across the country. I'll bet you don't talk at all but send little clicks, dots and dashes.... I'm right aren't I?" The foot shuffling and rising buzz from the adepts was a sure sign that he was hitting close. "I have an idea for you, I think I'll invent the telephone. Instead of the old clikkety-clack how would you like to *really* talk across the country? Speak into a gadget here and have your voice come out at the far end of the wire?"

The Hertug's piggy little eyes blinked greedily. "It is said that in the old days this could be done, but we have tried and have failed. Can you do this thing?"

"I can—if we can come to an agreement first. But before I make any promises I have to see your equipment."

This brought the usual groans of complaint about secrecy, but in the end avarice won over taboo and the door to the holy of holies was opened for Jason while two of the *sciuloj*, with bared and ready daggers, stood at his sides. At almost the same instant Jason looked in through the door he heard the sound.

Now the reaction of the human body, while remarkably fast, need certain finite measures of time and have been measured over and over again with a great deal of accuracy. The commands of the brain, speedy as they may be, must be carried by sluggish nerves and put into operation by inert lumps of muscle. Therefore to say that Jason's reactions were instantaneous is to tell a lie, or at least exaggerate. Only to his watchers did his actions appear to take place that fast; they were older, and less alert, and had not had the advantage of Pyrran survival training. So to their point of view the sacred portal was opened and Jason vanished in a flurry of activity. Two lightning blows sent his guardians spinning, and before they had fallen to the floor their supposed captive was through the door and it was slammed in their faces. Before the first dumfounded Persson could jump forward the bolt grated home inside and the door was sealed.

Things were a little more complex than that to Jason. When the door opened he had had a good view of the inside of the room, of a slave cranking the handle on a crude collection of junk that could only have been a generator. Thick wires looped across the room from the thing to a man who stood before some blades of copper pushing at them with a wooden stick, while above his head fat sparks leaped the gap between two brassy spheres. As if to complete this illustration for a bronze-age edition of "First Steps in Electricity" another cable twisted up from the spark gap and vanished out a small window. The entire thing might have been labeled "How to Generate A Radio Signal in the Crudest Manner." As Jason reached this conclusion in the smallest fraction of a second, and at almost the very same instant, he heard the sound.

What he heard could have been distant thunder, an earthquake, a volcano or some giant explosion. It rumbled and rolled, muffled by distance, yet still clear. It resembled none of these things to Jason, but made him think only of a high altitude rocket or jet, cleaving through the atmosphere.

It must have been the juxtaposition of these two things, occurring as they did at the same time, the view of a radio transmitter, no matter how crude, and the thought that there might be a civilized craft or some kind up there containing men who would come to his aid if he could only contact them. The idea was an insane one, but even as he realized that fact he was through the door and bolting it behind him. Perhaps he did it because he had been pushed around entirely too much and felt like pushing someone else for a change. In any case it was done, insane or not, and he might as well carry through.

The generator slave looked up, startled, but when Jason glanced at him he lowered his eyes and kept cranking. The man who had been working the transmitter spun about, startled by the slam of the door and the muffled pounding and shouts that followed instantly from the other side. He groped for his dagger when he saw the stranger, but before it was clear of the scabbard Jason was on him and after a few quick Pyrran infighting blows the man lost all interest in what was happening and slid to the floor. Jason straddled his body, picked the stick up, nodded to the slave who began cranking faster, and began to tap out a message.

S-O-S ... S-O-S ... he sent first, then as fragments of code came back to him he spelled out J-A-S-O-N D-A-L-T H-R-E.... N-E-E-D A-I-D.... R-I-C-H.... R-E-W-A-R-D ... F-O-R ... H-E-L-P....

He varied this a bit, repeated his name often, and tried other themes appealing for off-world aid. It was a slim chance that he had heard a rocket, and even slimmer chance that they would pick his message out of the static if they happened to be listening. He had no evidence that any off-worlders were in contact with this planet, merely hope. He tapped on and the slave ground away industriously. His arm was growing tired by the time the old guard in the other room found something heavy enough to swing and broke the door down. Jason stopped tapping and turned to face the apoplectic Hertug, rubbing his tired wrist.

"Your equipment works fine, though it could use a lot of improvements."

"Kill him.... Kill!" the Hertug sputtered.

"Kill me and there goes your *caroj*, as well as your telephone system and your only chance to wrap up all the industrial secrets in one big bundle," Jason said, looking around for something heavy to swing.

***

A gigantic explosion slammed into the room; a crack appeared in one wall and dust floated down from the ceiling. There was a sound of snapping small arms fire in the distance.

"It worked!" Jason shouted with unrestrained glee and hurled a heavy roll of wire at the startled men in the doorway and followed instantly after it in a headlong dive. There was a flurry of action, most of the damage being done by his boots, then he was through and running out of the throne room with the men bellowing in pursuit.

A small war seemed to be raging ahead, the sharp explosions of

121

gunfire being mixed with the heavier thud of bombs and grenades. Walls were down, doors blasted open while confused soldiers rushed in panic through the clouds of dust. One of them tried to stop Jason who kept on going, carrying the man's club with him. Sunlight shone ahead and he dived through a riven wall and landed, rolling in the open ground next to the dock. A spaceship's lifeboat stood there, still glowing hot from the speed of descent, and next to it stood Meta keeping up a continuous fire with her gun, happily juggling micro-grenades with her free hand.

"What were you waiting for," she snapped. "I have been in orbit over this planet for a month now, waiting for some word from you. There are dozens of radio transmitters on this continent and I have been monitoring them all." She fired a long burst at an upper story where some bowmen had been foolish enough to appear, then ran to Jason, eyes wet with tears. "Oh, darling, I was so worried."

She held him—with her grenade-throwing arm—and kissed him fiercely. She kept her eyes open while she was doing this but only had to fire once.

"Jason!" a voice called and Ijale appeared, half-supporting the still dazed Mikah.

"Who is this?" Meta snapped, the chill back in her voice.

"Why—just someone I know," Jason answered, smiling insincerely. "You should recognize the man, he's the one who arrested me."

"Here is a gun, you will want to kill him yourself."

Jason took the gun, but used it to clear a nearby roof-top, the powerful kick of the Pyrran automatic was like a caress on the heel of his hand.

"I don't think I want to kill him. He saved my life once, though he has tried to lose it for me a dozen times since. Let's get upstairs to the ship and I'll tell you about it. There are more healthy spots than this to have a conversation."

XII

Washed, shaved, scrubbed, cleaned, filled with good food and slightly awash with alcoholic drink, Jason collapsed into the acceleration couch and firmly swore that life was worth living after all.

"You can't appreciate the simple things of life until you have gone without them for a while. Or the better things either." He reached out and took Meta's hand. She pulled it away and fed more digits into the computer.

"How did you find me?" he asked, trying to discover a subject that she might warm to.

"That should be obvious. We saw the markings on the ship that took you away and charted a directional trace before it went into jump-space. We identified the markings and I went to Cassylia, but the ship had never arrived there. I back-tracked the straight-line course and found three possible planets near enough to have registered in the ship during jump-space flight. Two are highly organized with modern spaceports and would have known if the ship had landed. It hadn't. Therefore you must have forced the ship down on the planet we just left. And once you were there you would find one of the radios to send a message. Which is what you did. It is obvious. Who is she?" The final words were in a distinctly chillier tone of voice, and there could be only one she, Ijale, who crouched across the room, obviously unhappy and wide-eyed with fear at this voyage in a spaceship, not understanding the language the others spoke.

"I've told you before—just a friend. She was with us, and helped us, too. I couldn't let her go back to the life in the desert, it's more brutal than you can possibly imagine. There is an entire planetful of slaves back there, and of course I can't save them all. But I can do this much, take out the one person there who would rather see me live than die."

"What do you intend to do with her?" The sub-zero temperature of Meta's voice left no doubt as to what she wanted to do with her. Jason had already given this a good deal of thought, and if Ijale was going to live much longer she had to be separated as soon as possible from the deadly threat of female Pyrran jealousy.

"We stop at the next civilized planet and let her off. I have enough money to leave a deposit in a bank that will last her for years. Make arrangements for it to be paid out only a bit at a time, so no matter how she is cheated she will still have enough. I'm not going to worry about her, if she was able to survive in the *krenoj* legion she can get along well anywhere on a settled world."

He could hear the complaints on when he broke the news to Ijale, but it was for her own survival.

"I shall care for and lead her in the paths of righteousness," a remembered voice spoke from the doorway. Mikah stood there, clutching to the jamb, a turban of bandages on his head.

"That's a wonderful idea," Jason agreed enthusiastically. He turned to Ijale and spoke in her own language. "Did you hear that? Mikah is going to take you home with him and look after you. I'll arrange for some money to be paid to you for all your needs, he'll explain to you what money is. I want you to listen to him carefully, note exactly what he says, then do the exact opposite. You must promise me you will do that and never break your word. In that way you may make some mistakes and will be wrong sometimes, but all the rest of the time things will go very smoothly."

"I cannot leave you! Take me with you—I'll be your slave always!" she wailed.

"What did she say?" Meta snapped, catching some of the meaning.

"You are evil, Jason," Mikah declaimed, getting the needle back into the familiar groove. "She will obey you, I know that, so no matter how I labor she will always do as you say."

"I sincerely hope so," Jason said fervently. "One has to be born into your particular brand of illogic to get any pleasure from it. The rest of us are happier bending a bit under the impact of existence, and exacting a mite more pleasure from the physical life around us."

"Evil I say, and you shall not go unpunished." His hand appeared from behind the door jamb and it held a pistol that he had found below. "I am taking command of this ship. You will secure the two women so that they can cause no trouble, then we will proceed to Cassylia for your trial."

Meta had her back turned to Mikah and was sitting in the control chair a good five meters from him with her hands filled with navigational notes. She slowly raised her head and looked at Jason and a smile broke across her face.

"You said once you didn't want him killed."

"I still don't want him killed, but I also have no intention of going to Cassylia." He echoed her smile and turned away.

He sighed happily and there was a sudden rush of feet behind his back. No shots were fired but a hoarse scream, a thud and a sharp cracking noise told him that Mikah had lost his last argument.